TORCHWOOD

The Men Who
Sold the World

D0850934

New titles in the Torchwood *series from BBC Books:*

Long Time Dead *by Sarah Pinborough*

First Born *by James Goss*

The Men Who Sold the World *by Guy Adams*

TORCHWOOD

The Men Who Sold the World

Guy Adams

BOOKS

1 3 5 7 9 10 8 6 4 2

Published in 2011 by BBC Books, an imprint of Ebury Publishing.
A Random House Group Company

Copyright © Guy Adams 2011

Guy Adams has asserted his right to be identified as the author of this
Work in accordance with the Copyright, Designs and Patents Act 1988

Torchwood is a BBC Worldwide Production for the BBC and Starz Originals.
Executive producers: Russell T Davies, Julie Gardner and Jane Tranter

Original series created by Russell T Davies,
and developed and produced by BBC Cymru Wales.
BBC, 'Torchwood' and the Torchwood logo are trademarks of
the British Broadcasting Corporation and are used under licence.

The Random House Group Limited Reg. No. 954009

Addresses for companies within the Random House Group can be found at
www.randomhouse.co.uk

A CIP catalogue record for this book is available from the British Library.

ISBN 978 1 849 90285 4

MIX
Paper from
responsible sources
FSC® C016897

The Random House Group Limited supports the Forest Stewardship
Council® (FSC®), the leading international forest certification
organisation. All our titles that are printed on Greenpeace approved
FSC® certified paper carry the FSC® logo. Our paper procurement
policy can be found at www.randomhouse.co.uk/environment

Editorial director: Albert DePetrillo
Editorial manager: Nicholas Payne
Series editor: Steve Tribe
Cover design: Lee Binding © Woodlands Books Ltd, 2011
Production: Rebecca Jones

Printed and bound in Great Britain by CPI Cox & Wyman, Reading, RG1 8EX

To buy books by your favourite authors and register for offers,
visit www.randomhouse.co.uk

100,000 BC

Bent Low sniffed the air and moved out onto the plain. The sun was dropping in the sky, and Bent Low knew the night chill would rob him of his breath if he stayed out much longer. It was colder these days than it used to be. The air made smoke grow in front of Bent Low's face when he breathed. He would try and catch the smoke, squeeze the warmth from it. But the smoke was only the ghost of fire, and ghosts held no warmth for Bent Low. If he wasn't back in the cave by the time the sun broke on the earth, back next to the fire that still lived, he would die out here. And that would feed his family no better than the empty pouch on his back.

Bent Low remembered when his father had brought home meat from the plain, there had always been plenty of it. Bent Low's father had been a great hunter. Perhaps he had been too good. Perhaps his axe had killed all of the animals so that now, as Bent Low tried to feed his own family, there was nothing left to eat.

Bent Low kept his eyes on the dirt, reading the story of the earth, the route the animals had taken as they also came onto the plain looking for food. He saw the track of an ox, like two curled mouths. It was a sign of good food. But he did not trust it. He had followed the tracks of oxen for hours before and found nothing. The earth held the story of the oxen's passing for too long since the last rain. They had been gone for many days. The ground told him things that were not so. The ground stole the food from his family's belly. He took his knife and hacked at the ground. Sometimes, when you were angry enough, the earth gave up roots and bulbs. The ground feared your knife. It tried to make friends with you so you would not kill it. The gifts of the earth were not as good as meat but they were better than nothing at all.

As he cut at the earth there was the sound of thunder from the horizon. He looked at the sky, trying to decide whether it was angry or pleased with him. It was a cold sky and kept its feelings to itself. He looked towards where the noise had been. There was something there, a new shape on the horizon. He shouldn't look, he had no time. If he waited any longer the darkness would come and kill him with its cold.

But Bent Low was curious. Bent Low wondered if the sky had given him a gift.

Bent Low ran towards the shape in the distance, forcing his tired legs to move fast so they gave him speed and heat.

As he got closer, he could see that the shape was a man, though not like Bent Low. This man's skin was darker but almost hairless. He was bigger than Bent Low, a giant, and he wore strange, thin skins. He will be dead when the cold comes, thought Bent Low. Those skins will give no heat at all. Maybe he was dead already. For surely a man could not fall out of the sky and survive?

'Please,' the man said, though Bent Low could not understand the noise, keeping back in case the man was dangerous. 'Please get help...' the man continued, reaching out to Bent Low. 'My name's... Rex Matheson, and I'm with the CIA.'

One

Wilson had thrown up so often on the voyage out he was sure this must be soul he was picking from between his teeth. Though having worked eighteen years for the Department, it was unlikely he had any soul left.

There was a knock on his cabin door. He rolled his cheek from the lip of the toilet and went to answer it.

'Yanks are here, sir,' said the junior rating outside before offering a salute.

'At ease sailor.' Wilson smiled. Another six months and the boy would be spitting on the security services, not saluting them. 'I'll be right up.'

Wilson closed the door and headed back to the bathroom.

He looked at his face in the mirror. It was as grey and wet as offal.

Why couldn't he just sit behind a desk? The last five years had been a gastric diary of seasick oceans, far-eastern belly pains and oriental fevers.

He bet Yates didn't have to put up with so much travel. But then Rick Yates was like most Foreign Secretaries: you had to explain the lingo to them the minute they were beyond the Central Line.

The cabin shook as the American boat pulled alongside, and Wilson stepped out of his cabin before the renewed rocking set his stomach off again. On these little boats you felt every damn wave.

It was beginning to get dark, but the evening held its heat. Climbing into the open air was like sticking your head under an electric hand-dryer.

'Bloody wonderful,' Wilson muttered as he felt his forehead erupt with sweat. 'Absolutely bloody wonderful.' He waddled over to Harris, the Navy officer in charge. 'Evening, Commander,' he said. 'How many are there?'

'Four above deck,' Commander Harris replied. 'If our intelligence is accurate, that would leave three more below. Typical covert vehicle, no insignia, non-military. Shows they're being cautious, at least. How do you want to play this?'

Wilson shrugged. 'Quickly. The sooner we're bound for friendly waters the better. I'll show off the cargo, you and your men keep an eye out up here.'

'I'll have a couple of men accompany you to the hold. You shouldn't be on your own with Gleason.'

'What's he going to do? He's a collection agent, nothing more.' Wilson's standing orders were to limit the number of people who saw what they were carrying. That included the Navy. 'You keep your men up here. The only threats that need concern us are gatecrashers.'

The Commander looked displeased but nodded, and the two men crossed the deck to where the boats were being joined by a gangway.

'Good evening,' said Wilson, as the four men climbed aboard. Dear Lord, he thought, look at them in their crewcuts and cargo pants, they couldn't have looked more like soldiers if they'd turned up in dress uniform. He extended his hand to the man in front. 'Glad you found us all right.'

The man stared at him, a scowl beneath a thin bristle of salt and pepper hair, but didn't reply.

'Fine,' Wilson said. 'I can dispense with pleasantries.' He withdrew his hand and gestured beneath deck. 'This way, Colonel Gleason.' Wilson smiled at the faint surprise on the older man's face. 'We read our files,' he said. 'I wasn't about to loiter here without having a good idea of who I was meeting.' He gestured to each of them in turn. 'Oscar Lupé, Owen Mills, Glen Shaeffer. I presume the rest of your unit is still aboard your boat? I believe in knowing who I'm dealing with, Colonel. You did the same, I'm sure.'

'Actually,' Gleason replied, 'I didn't bother.'

Touché, Wilson admitted, leading the Americans below deck.

When they came to the hold's heavy iron door, Wilson tapped out the key-code to the lock. There was the solid clunk of an iron bolt withdrawing and a hiss of air as the door opened.

'After you,' said Wilson, ushering the Americans inside.

Stepping through the door after them, he pressed the button for the lights, and held back as the fluorescents came on. They illuminated four packing crates sat a neat distance from each other. Each bore a distinctive logo on them, a 'T' built from hexagons. Wilson took a crowbar from a hook on the wall and marched over, swinging it nonchalantly from one hand to the other.

'Here you are, gentlemen,' he announced. 'Ordnance several light years beyond your current defence programme.' He handed the crowbar to Lupé. 'In fact, beyond *anyone's* current defence programme. All guaranteed one of a kind. Certainly in this arm of the universe.'

Lupé prised the top off one of the cases and stood back so that Gleason could inspect the contents. He pulled out a gun made of a deep red metal.

'Do be careful with that, Colonel,' said Wilson. 'That's a Judoon firearm. At its highest setting it would punch a hole through the side of this ship and we'd all be swimming home.'

Gleason examined the gun and then tossed it back nodding for Lupé to open another crate. There was the squeal of nails wrenched from wood and then Gleason was poking through thin, straw-like packing material while Lupé opened the other two crates.

'Obviously the manifest is as reported to your superiors,' said Wilson, eager to conclude his business.

Gleason glanced at him. 'It's my job to make sure,' he said. 'That's why my government didn't bother sending an office clerk.'

'Sir.' Shaeffer was holding a large rifle that appeared to be encrusted in shellfish.

'You had a leak?' Gleason asked Wilson, stepping towards the other man.

'It's bio-organic,' Wilson explained as Shaeffer began tugging at fronds of seaweed that hung from the rifle's midsection. 'It's supposed to look like that. Look, do be careful, all of this equipment is—'

The rifle gave a small cough, and Lupé vanished. The crowbar he had been holding fell to the ground and bounced, the clang of metal against metal echoing around the hold.

Gleason pulled out his sidearm and pointed it towards Wilson.

'Don't you bloody point that at me,' Wilson shouted. 'Your man activated it by mistake.' The rifle continued to hum. 'You need to put that down!' he insisted to Shaeffer who was now holding the rifle at arm's length.

The soldier looked to Gleason, who nodded. Carefully, he placed it on the floor. It continued to hum, a faint orange light working its way up and down its length.

'What do we do, sir?' Shaeffer asked Gleason.

'You back away from the crates,' said Wilson, 'and we figure out how your commanding officer is going to explain the disappearance of one of his men due to negligence.'

'The negligence,' said Gleason, 'is in your people not storing the weapons securely.'

'Your man started playing with it!' insisted Wilson. 'That's hardly our fault.' He sighed. 'Look, this doesn't need to get out of hand.'

Gleason stared at the sidearm in his hand. 'Thing is,' he said, 'I don't like being on the thin end of this deal. Under-informed and one man down, just because you guys like to feel superior. I got to think to myself: what's the best way forward for me and my men?' He nodded to himself. 'Yeah, that's what I got to think...'

He pulled the trigger and shot Wilson in the head.

'Door,' he said, nodding at Mills. He scratched at his grey crewcut as the soldier ran towards the heavy metal door and bolted it shut.

'What the hell, Colonel?' Shaeffer shouted.

'Soldier,' said Gleason, 'I hear one more word out of you, you'll be as dead as him.' He gestured towards Wilson. 'It's down to you that I'm thinking on my goddamned feet here.'

'How was I supposed to—'

Gleason charged at Shaeffer, grabbing him by the throat and slamming him against the bulkhead. He forced the barrel of his sidearm into the man's mouth. 'I'm serious, soldier!' he bellowed. 'Shut up, OK?'

Shaeffer nodded, his teeth clicking against the metal of the gun barrel.

Lieutenant Colonel Mulroney was sat below deck on the American boat, the remaining members of the platoon, Sergeants Joe Leonard and David Ellroy, alongside him.

When his radio crackled, Mulroney grabbed it quickly. 'Sir?'

'You're on,' said Gleason's voice. 'Assume you're expected and mind the damn hold.'

'Roger that.' Mulroney grabbed his rifle and turned to Leonard and Ellroy. 'OK, boys, we're ball-deep even quicker than usual, let's go to the rescue, shall we?'

When Commander Harris heard the gunshot he knew that his instincts not to trust the Americans had been right.

'Be ready,' he shouted, raising his rifle. 'Sounds like our visitors have turned nasty.'

He detailed four of his men below deck while he led the rest of his limited company towards the gangplank adjoining the ships. Damn the security service and it's bloody secrecy, he thought. I should have a full complement of men and the support of the Navy at my back. Not a handful of young ratings and no idea of what we're defending. *You're defending your lives*, came a quiet voice inside his head, just as he saw a small object sail above their heads. *Oh God...*

'Grenade!' he shouted, as its metal casing bounced off the side of the boat with a *clang*.

The explosion ripped out a chunk of the bridge and sent several men screaming overboard. Harris had run towards stern the moment he'd seen the grenade, hoping to outdistance the worst of the blast. He felt the heat lift him from his feet and push him through the air. He clutched his rifle tight to his chest and rolled with the momentum as he hit the deck. Skidding against the railings, he lifted his rifle with shaking arms and pointed it past the fire and smoke to the other boat. His head buzzed, ears whining. He could smell burning hair, probably his own.

A couple of shapes moved beyond the smoke, and a pair of zip-lines snaked across from the Americans' boat to their own. Yeah, thought Harris, not that bloody clever, are you? Took out the gangway, you stupid, sloppy bastards.

As soon as a shape appeared on the line, he fired at it. His aim was off, his arms shaking, his vision blurred and unreliable. A spray of machine-gunfire came from the American boat. Mopping up, Harris thought. Killing my boys. He tried to aim his rifle again, sure he saw one of the yanks walking towards him. He blacked out for a moment. When he opened his eyes, the setting sun was almost entirely blocked out by a figure standing over him.

'Any survivors?' an American voice called from the other end of the boat.

'No,' said the man standing over him. For a moment, Harris thought the man had mistaken him for dead. Then, as the shadow raised a handgun towards him and pulled the trigger, he realised the man hadn't been mistaken at all.

Gleason was sat on the lip of one of the packing crates as the muffled noise of a grenade explosion above them was followed by gunfire. Shaeffer was still standing with his back against the bulkhead, apparently frozen by his commanding officer's actions.

'What are we going to do, Colonel?' asked Mills,

a young kid from the Midwest who was still new enough at this to think he was about God's work.

From beyond the door came the sound of more gunfire. Three quick bursts then silence.

'We're going to take what we came for,' Gleason replied as his radio crackled in his hand.

'All clear, sir,' said Mulroney's voice. 'What's the code?'

'JF323B,' Gleason told him.

'Check,' came the reply, followed by three electronic bleeps and the clunk of the door unlocking. Mulroney stepped inside. 'We're good to go,' he said.

'Then let's get on with it,' said Gleason. 'But treat the crates carefully, they're not secure.'

'Great,' Mulroney replied. 'Hey, where's Lupé?'

Shaeffer looked nervously towards Gleason. The older man shook his head. 'God alone knows.'

American Airlines flight AA2010 was two hours out of Fort Worth. Captain Roger Walker turned to his First Officer, Janice Albright, smiled, and imagined the two of them under Cancun sunshine. Then he imagined Janice's husband sat on a sun-lounger between them, and the mental image turned sour.

'About half an hour till we land,' he said, brushing a few crumbs of tuna wrap off his chest. 'Just catch happy hour.'

'Every hour's happy on your salary,' Janice replied with a smile.

'I'll buy the first round then,' said Roger, pretending not to notice the slight twinge of discomfort on Janice's face as he leaned closer. 'I know how to show a girl a good time.'

He leaned back in his seat and tried to think of something innocuous to fill the awkward silence left by his clumsy flirtation. He had just struck on the idea of mentioning the recent reshuffle of the long-haul roster (as close to verbal paint-drying as he could imagine) when they were both startled by the sudden appearance of Oscar Lupé.

The man was embedded in the flight controls in front of them, a single clenching hand outstretched towards Roger.

'Inside me,' the soldier said, his voice cracking. 'Feel it inside me.'

'Jesus!' screamed Roger. 'Where the hell did he—'

Which was all he managed before the Boeing 747 with its full complement of passengers went into free fall and such questions were pushed far away.

Two

There are many pleasurable things a man can do in Nassau. A lot of them involve oil, sunshine and staring at beautiful people in swimwear. If the pleasure of the sands palls, there are restaurants, bars and a casino where the aforementioned beautiful people go to lose all their money in nice surroundings. One thing you will never find recommended is sitting in the back of a white van surrounded by enough electrical equipment to stock a small branch of Radio Shack. This is because vans, as large metal boxes, are extremely stupid things to sit in while the sun shines. The only people unfortunate enough to do it are pool-cleaning contractors and CIA operatives pretending to be pool-cleaning contractors.

'What the hell have you been eating in here?' Rex sniffed again, the need to pin down this odour going beyond self-preservation. 'Boiled sneakers?'

'I had a wrap earlier,' Ted replied.

'A wrap? What sort of wrap? Fried goat?' Rex snorted deep. 'I think I actually bruised my nose, it'll bleed in a minute. Seriously, your smell is that bad.'

'My smell? How do you know it's me?'

'Because I'm a civilised son of a bitch and I only just got here.' Rex shook his head, 'Unbelievable, like someone stood in a dead guy and tracked it in.'

'I can't smell anything.'

'Burned out your glands. Probably never smell again.'

'So let me get out, get some fresh air.'

'OK, but you make it quick and keep out of sight. The Russians see a fat white boy in a cheap suit they're going to know the CIA's in town.'

'Screw you.'

Ted stepped outside, and Rex snatched at the brief guff of fresh air before the doors closed again.

'Ambrosia,' he said.

He lifted the headphones and placed one ear to them. There was the second-hand sound of tinny gangsta rap. A weedy Russian voice attempting to sing along.

'You're so cool, Dmitri,' said Rex. 'If only your friends in St Petersburg could hear you now.'

Dmitri Lakhonin's 'friends' were the Ukrainian Boiko family, major players in the heroin trade. The CIA had decided to groom Lakhonin as a potential source of intelligence. Intelligence in the espionage sense, of course – you only had to hear him sing to realise the word wouldn't be appropriate any other way.

Rex wrapped the headphones around his neck

and reached for a magazine Ted had discarded. He kept one ear on Dmitri as he flicked through its pages. There was nothing worth reading, movie stars and fashions. He peeled out a sample sachet of aftershave and slipped it into his pocket. He had established that Ted had no interest in improving body odour, so it would be a waste to leave it. There was the sound of knocking from the headphones, and Rex tipped his head slightly to listen. Dmitri switched off the music.

'Who is it?' he asked in highly accented English.

'Room service,' a voice replied, chuckling.

Rex pulled the headphones on. Since when did room service find itself funny? He heard the sound of a semi-automatic being racked and guessed Dmitri was wondering the same thing. Either that or the turndown service put him on edge.

The bedroom door opened, and Rex heard a Bahamian voice: 'Here you are, my friend. I bring her safe and sound, yes? You got a nice tip for me?'

Rex sighed. Looked like Dmitri had ordered up some company. If there was one thing worse than listening to the man's singing... There was a rustle of paper as money was exchanged and the door closed.

'Hey, honey,' Dmitri said, now alone with the girl. 'You got some sugar for Daddy?'

There was no reply, and Rex began to feel uncomfortable. Something about this wasn't right.

'You're beautiful,' said Dmitri. 'Really beautiful.

How old are you?'

The answer was quiet, barely even registered by the microphone.

Rex sat there for a moment, a shiver running through him before he yanked off the headphones, opened the back of the van and ran towards the hotel.

Rex forced himself to stop running when he entered the hotel lobby. This was bad enough, without making a public scene. He moved towards the elevators and hit the call button, grinding the toes of his shoes against the marble tiles of the lobby floor. 'Come on, come on...'

He watched as the counter worked its way down.

The doors opened. A solitary man stood inside. He was well dressed but local. What the hell, Rex thought, I might as well *really* screw this up.

'You just seen Dmitri in room 1204?' he asked as the man made to step past him. The surprised look on the man's face was reflected in the elevator's mirrored walls and more than enough evidence for Rex.

He smiled his best 'absolutely not up to anything' smile, glanced around to make sure nobody was watching, punched the pimp in the throat and stepped after him into the elevator. He pressed the button for the twelfth floor, the pimp clutching at his throat and wheezing. Rex brought his knee up into the man's face and grabbed him by the scruff of the neck to stop him falling to the floor.

'Stay with me,' he said. 'We're going back upstairs.'

The pimp took a thin breath and reached inside his jacket. Rex thought that was a bad idea, shoving him back against the mirrored wall of the elevator. He stepped in close so the pimp didn't have room to extend his arms, especially the one that likely now had a weapon at the end of it. Rex grabbed the wrist inside the pimp's jacket and pulled out the man's hand.

'What have we got?' he asked, glancing at the counter that showed the elevator was nearly at the twelfth floor.

The pimp was holding a small switchblade. Rex pulled a back-handed slap across the man's face and then reached for the knife, twisting back the man's little finger to get it. There was a crack and the pimp cried out. Rex slipped the knife, hilt-first, up the left-hand sleeve of his suit jacket, holding it in place with his little finger. With his right hand he yanked the pimp in front of him as the elevator arrived at the twelfth floor.

'Stand up straight,' said Rex. 'If you look nice and presentable when that door opens, I might not kill you.'

The doors opened and a cheerful bell sounded along an empty corridor. Rex looked over the pimp's shoulder, giving the shaking man a smile.

'Don't worry, I could tell you were trying. Back to 1204.'

Rex pushed him out of the elevator, reaching for the handgun that he would avoid using if possible.

'Knock,' he told the pimp once they were outside Dmitri's door. 'Quickly. Tell him you need to come in.'

The pimp did as he was told.

Inside they could hear Dmitri swearing as he came to answer the door.

'What?' he asked, opening the door a crack. Rex shoved the pimp forward so that the door swung open and Dmitri fell backwards, the weight of the pimp knocking him to the floor. Rex kept moving, wanting to overwhelm Dmitri before he could use the loaded gun he knew the man would be holding. He had underestimated Dmitri's speed – the gun was up and firing before Rex had even cleared the doorway. The pimp took the shot, losing his ear and what remained of his cool.

Rex fired as the pimp started screaming. A small red dot appeared in Dmitri's forehead, and his rapping skills and sexual preferences splattered over the wall behind him. Rex brought the handle of his revolver down on the back of the pimp's head, closed the door and sat on the edge of the bed for a second, wondering how best to deal with this.

The sound of crying intruded on his thoughts. In the corner of the room, huddled and afraid, sat a young Bahamian girl.

Rex holstered his gun, and dropped the pimp's switchblade into his jacket pocket. He yanked a blanket off the bed and walked over to the girl. He draped the blanket around her, wrapping it several times to try and cover her tiny body.

'It's going to be OK,' he said to her. Though he

was damned if he knew quite how.

He walked over to a standard lamp that stood in the corner of the room, stuck his head beneath the lampshade and said, 'As you may have guessed, we have a slight problem.'

'A slight problem?' Rex winced at Esther's slight air of panic in his phone headset. 'A dead asset, a pimp with concussion and a 12-year old with years of therapy ahead of her?'

'Less now,' Rex said.

'Not to mention a high-class hotel room now in need of a deep clean.'

'Not that high-class.'

'I couldn't afford it, so it's high-class to me. Luckily, we think the hotel owner wants to be friends with the United States.'

'Wants paying to let us bug his damn rooms, you mean. Listen I'll get enough crap today from people way above your pay grade, so if you've quite finished?' He felt slightly guilty at the couple of beats of silence in his ear, but Esther Drummond was easy to dominate and he really wasn't in the mood.

'Watch Analysts are people too,' she said.

Trying to turn it all into a joke, thought Rex, not wanting any suggestion of there being an issue. Next will come the friendly reassurance.

'This'll blow over. You'll be golden boy again soon enough.'

'Damn right,' Rex replied with a smile at how easy he found it to predict her. 'A genius like me can rule the world.'

'Want to prove it?'

Rex could hear the shift in Esther's tone. This was going to be good. 'What have you got for me?'

'Officially? Not so much. Unofficially?'

Rex sighed. 'OK, talk to me.'

'You know Penelope?'

'Penelope who?'

'Lupé. She's worked here for a few years, doesn't matter. It's about her husband, Oscar.'

'This isn't starting well...'

'Patience! He was CIA too, S.O.G.'

'Special Operations? I don't want to know...'

'He's dead.'

'Not the first, won't be the last.'

'He died in a plane crash. A plane he wasn't scheduled to fly on in fact, wait... I can go one better than that – a plane he *wasn't* flying on.'

'That makes a lot of sense.'

'I've sent video to your phone, lifted from the flight-deck camera. Watch it.'

Rex pulled his phone out of his jacket and scrolled through to his email. He double-tapped the video file. The footage was silent, the two pilots going casually about their work, checking readings, flipping switches, chatting. All of a sudden, a shadow was cast across the flight deck as something appeared in shot. Squinting at the small screen, Rex could just make out the upper body of a man now hanging in front of the two panicking pilots.

'What the hell?'

'Freaky, huh?' said Esther in his ear.

'H.A.L.O. jump?'

'No way. Throw a man at the nosecone of a Boeing cruising at 45,000 feet and he would make a dent, yes, maybe even crack the glass. But he wouldn't end up embedded in the instrument panel. And he stayed there, right up to when the plane hit the water.'

'So how did it happen?'

'Who knows? It's completely beyond anyone's best guess. Even if he had been shot through the glass of the windscreen, the loss of pressure would have sucked him straight back out again. Interested?'

'Intrigued, but what's it got to do with us? If he died on S.O.G. business, they don't need me poking around.'

'Unofficially, his unit's gone off the map. When the flight dropped out of the sky, we flagged it as possible terrorist action. S.O.G.'s not talking – nothing new there – but in the meantime Penelope's left wondering what happened to her husband and the 450 passengers on flight AA2010.'

'I sympathise but, still, what business is this of Clandestine?'

'The S.O.G. unit are still out there and look intent on causing more fatalities.'

'I'm listening.'

'Penelope had a phone call...'

Mr Wynter wakes to a glorious morning. He steps out onto the front porch. Fresh sun hits old bones, and he thinks it's like the touch of God. Picking up his copy of the *Washington Times*, he heads back inside to brew coffee. The name on the newspaper delivery label is not Wynter. But then Mr Wynter is not a man constrained by names.

While the coffee machine percolates, he skims through the leader articles and microwaves a bowl of oatmeal. He eats his oatmeal with syrup. It is an indulgence, but Mr Wynter is a believer in giving in to indulgences. Without indulgence, life can seem endless.

Next door, the volume on the TV is turned up loud and the windows are open. The fat librarian who lives there is watching *Good Morning America*. It feels like George Stephanopoulos is sharing his damned oatmeal. Mr Wynter does not watch the morning news programmes. He knows better. He doesn't close his own windows either, that would be a concession, and he does not tolerate those anywhere near as much as indulgences.

After breakfast, he does half an hour on the treadmill. Nothing too drastic, a fast walk for a couple of miles. He listens to Benny Goodman loud enough to drown out next door's TV and imagines a smaller world. A world where, as a black man blows into a trumpet in Carnegie Hall, a dictator invades Poland and plans the eradication of all but his master race. It is a simple world, he thinks. Not his world.

He switches off the treadmill and takes a shower. He looks at his old, old body in the bathroom mirror and remembers when it wasn't covered in liver spots. He remembers when the skin didn't hang off him. It looks like it's melting, pouring off him, like the skin poured off the men in the jungles of Vietnam all those years ago.

He is selecting his clothes for the day, fawn slacks and a cream-coloured shirt, when the phone rings. He answers it, giving an irritated glance through his bedroom window towards next door where the TV is as loud as ever. He can see the big plasma screen flickering through the net drapes that hang in the fat librarian's windows. It's advertising Japanese motor cars.

'Yes.'

'Mr Wynter, I'm afraid we have a situation.'

Wynter listens for a few minutes and then replaces the receiver with a polite 'thank you'.

He puts away his fawn slacks and cream shirt. Today will not be the day he had expected. He takes out his light-grey three-piece, a tie and a white cotton shirt. Today is a day for uniform. It will also be a day for travelling, so he packs his small black holdall with a change of clothes (an identical change of clothes so really no change at all) and his washbag.

Next door, the TV continues to shout while Mr Wynter selects a book to take on his journey. He picks *Heart of Darkness* by Joseph Conrad. He has read it many times, but it fits neatly into his jacket pocket.

He calls for a car to take him to the airport. The car will be fifteen minutes.

He sits at his kitchen table, the sound of next door's TV still seeping through, even though he has now closed and locked his windows in preparation to leave.

He checks his watch. Still ten minutes until the car arrives.

He gets up, takes a small parcel from his holdall and slips it into his pocket. He leaves his holdall on the kitchen table and walks next door.

He knocks on the door. Loudly because of the goddamned TV.

'Yes?' The fat librarian answers, scooting her cat out of the way with a slippered foot. She pulls her house coat tighter (the belt bisecting her fat like string around a joint of beef) and looks at him suspiciously. But not that suspiciously, because he is just an old man in a grey suit.

'I'm from next door,' says Mr Wynter, cradling his left arm and wincing as if in pain. 'I fell. I think I broke my arm.'

The fat librarian's face wobbles into life. 'Oh, you poor thing!'

'I wondered if I might be able to use your phone? Mine seems to be dead.' Mr Wynter offers a pained smile. 'Knowing me, I forgot to pay the bill. My memory's not what it was.'

'Of course, honey,' says the fat librarian. 'Come in, come in.'

Mr Wynter does so, reaching behind him to close the door. As she walks over towards the phone, he reaches into his jacket pocket and opens the small case he has put there. Pulling out a syringe, he plunges the needle into her fat ass and steps back as she spins around flailing those thick arms of hers.

'What was...' She falls onto her baby-shit brown carpet, eyes wide and staring.

He doesn't bother to answer. Just watches as she lies there, the chemical working its way through her bloodstream. She gives a sudden, spastic thrash, her back arching against the carpet, her house coat falling open to show him the sort of flesh he hasn't glimpsed for many long years.

Finally she is still. When examined, it will look to all but the deepest of toxicological examinations as if she has died from a heart attack. Mr Wynter pulls on some gloves and turns the TV volume down on the remote. He leaves it at what he considers a sensible level; he is not, after all, an unreasonable man. The cat meows from where it watches him through the uprights of the stair rail. He checks his watch. Still plenty of time. He goes back into the kitchen and searches through the fat librarian's cupboards until he finds the kibble. He fills the cat's bowl, replaces the sack of food and lets himself out.

No need to be cruel.

Three

Angelo sat in the long grass and watched the Hernandez House. All the years he had known it – which wasn't many, but time moves with greater weight for a 12-year-old – it had remained empty. His mother said it had once belonged to a rich family, had been a place of parties and music that had gone on late into the night. Then the revolution had hounded them out and the building became home to crumbling stone, graffiti and splintered window shutters.

It sat in overgrown grounds, surrounded by a wall designed to keep people out but better at encouraging children in. There's nothing kids love more than a 'Keep Out' sign. Of course, people said it was haunted. People of a certain age always did. Whenever he mentioned the place to his grandmother, she would suck on the damp end of her cigar and cross herself. 'It is a house of devils,' she would say around fat, blue golf balls of tobacco smoke. 'To go there is to stain your soul.' But then Angelo's grandmother thought everything stained

your soul, so Angelo didn't take her warnings
seriously. Nor did he think the Hernandez House
was a house of devils. Though *something* had
recently taken up residence there.

The night before, Angelo had lain in his bed
listening to his grandmother's TV. She was deaf,
so she turned it up loud enough to shake the walls.
She liked action movies, so the walls shook a lot.

Despite the TV, he had heard the sound of a truck
coming down the track towards the Hernandez
House. He knew his grandmother wouldn't hear
it, she was too distracted by the adventures of Vin
Diesel or – her favourite – Wesley Snipes. 'Siempre
se apuesta por negro!' she would cry when she saw
one of his movies listed in the TV Guide.

Angelo had got out of bed and peered over the
windowsill of his room. The truck was driving
slowly down the track. Likely they thought that
nobody would see them. Most people thought
Angelo's grandmother's house was as derelict as
the mansion. In truth, she'd just let the place go.
There were no other houses around.

Angelo had watched the truck stop outside the
gates of the Hernandez House. A man had jumped
out, ran to the gates, opened them and then stood
back to let the truck drive through. Once clear the
man had swung the gates closed and begun to wind
a length of chain around the bars to lock them.
'The way to keep something safe is not to shout
about it,' Angelo had whispered, but knew that
this bit of wisdom would be lost on the stranger by
the gates. Truth was, a big padlock just told the
world that there was something worth stealing.

Tomorrow, he had thought, I'll see if I can find out what it is.

Now, having spent an hour or so chasing snakes in the grass, he wasn't so sure he wanted to know. He figured these people were hiding. You wouldn't live in a place like that unless you didn't want to be found. That was OK, Angelo often didn't want to be found either. He wouldn't tell. But he wouldn't get too close. Hidden people were usually scared, and scared people could get angry.

Shaeffer sat on the closed lid of the toilet and weighed the phone up in his hand. If Gleason caught him with it, he honestly didn't know what the man would do. He'd never doubted his commanding officer before. Gleason's rage was usually pointed squarely towards the enemy. But 'the enemy' no longer had the simple definition it used to have.

He tapped on the phone's screen, scrolling through the photos of Oscar and his wife, Penelope. Pictures of them laughing, kissing, raising their glasses towards the lens. Oscar felt like a spy, looking down on them from the veered perspective of the photographer's outstretched right hand.

Oscar shouldn't have kept his phone with him. It was against orders. Shaeffer proved why as he scrolled through the dead man's life. Everything from his taste in music and TV shows to messages from friends and family. The phone was a window onto its owner. And the longer that Shaeffer looked, the more he realised he hadn't known Oscar at all. We all hide behind masks, he thought, in this game more than any other. But if I wasn't looking at Oscar's face in these photos, I'd swear this phone belonged to someone else entirely. Someone happy and normal. Someone with Gloria Frigging Estefan on their Favourites playlist.

The phone had been in Oscar's bag. Gleason had made it Shaeffer's responsibility to clear away Oscar's stuff, dumping it over the side of the boat as they sailed away from the scene of the crime.

The scene of the crime... Jesus what had they become?

Shaeffer wasn't a stranger to moral grey areas. His career had been built on acts he couldn't comfortably discuss. But however bad it got, however much blood ended up on his hands, he had always been able to convince himself that he was acting for the greater good. That they were the grunts who got their hands dirty so that others could sleep safely at night.

He stared at a photo of Oscar and Penelope, heads pressed together, the familiar shape of Manhattan bridge over her shoulder. They gazed at the camera as a Brooklyn sun warmed their cheeks. Had Oscar ever told Penelope about the things they'd seen and done? About the villages they had left burning in Afghanistan, the bodies they had sent floating down the Hari? No. Shaeffer looked at the smiling face of the woman resting her head against Oscar's and decided that she knew nothing. People only looked that happy in the company of heroes.

He wondered whether the Company had contacted her yet. Whether they had manufactured a hero's death. He wondered whether the weight in his chest would lift, if only for a few seconds, if he were to tell her the truth.

He scrolled through the menu options to the phone's contacts, thumbing his way down the list until he saw Penelope's name. He let his finger hover over it for a few seconds then, hearing movement in the corridor outside the bathroom, he locked the phone's controls and tucked it away in his pocket.

'Shaeffer.' Mulroney's voice. 'You in there?'

'Yeah.'

'Well, finish up and get downstairs. The Colonel wants to talk to everybody.'

'OK.'

Shaeffer waited until he heard Mulroney's boots heading back up the hallway, gave it another thirty seconds, flushed and went downstairs.

He stepped into the front room where the rest of the unit were waiting.

There was little furniture, just a few chairs that someone had dragged from other parts of the house. The plaster had fallen away from sections of the walls, revealing the thin, wooden ribs of the building beneath. The air smelled wet. The floor felt soft.

'Here he is,' laughed Ellroy. 'Finished your chemical warfare?'

'Sit down,' said Gleason, nodding to a spare chair. Shaeffer did so, trying his best to look relaxed, to look like a guy that wasn't having doubts about the company he kept.

'OK,' said Gleason. 'So I've been thinking.'

'Which means this is serious,' joked Mulroney, the only man in the room who could do so without being shot.

'I guess it is,' said Gleason, with a half-smile. 'But, you know, the more I think about it, the more I think we're looking at an opportunity here. How many years have we been doing this? Dicked around by the moveable "moral compass" of whichever suit currently leads the thinking in global policy. We've all left friends in the desert somewhere. We've all wondered when what we did might make a difference.'

Gleason looked at each of his men in turn.

He shrugged. 'Maybe I'm just getting old, but the certainty in command I used to feel is gone. I just don't believe in what we do any more. Yesterday was the perfect example, putting our necks on the line for something that's going to spend the next few years being poked at by men in white coats.'

'You think it really is what they say, sir?' asked Mills. 'You think that stuff's alien?'

'Who knows?' Gleason replied. 'That's not the point. We weren't briefed, we weren't *warned*, and because of that one of our own dies.' He looked to Shaeffer, wanting to see how the man reacted. Predictably enough, the soldier was squirming in his chair. 'Well, that's enough. I'm drawing the line.'

'You suggesting what I think you're suggesting?' asked Mulroney. 'We going rogue here?'

'Too late to ask that,' said Leonard. 'We're off the grid already.'

'We could still come back from this,' said Ellroy. 'Come up with some excuse for the radio silence.'

'And stealing several crates of weaponry?' Leonard replied. 'Don't be an idiot, there'll be a kill order out on us already.'

'Maybe so,' said Gleason. 'But I'd like to see them implement it once we crack open those crates and start fighting back.'

'Use that stuff against our own?' asked Mills.

'It wouldn't be the first time,' Gleason replied, glancing again at Shaeffer. 'But I'm hoping it won't come to that. At the same time, I ain't talking about just sitting here and waiting for them. That's never been my style.' He smiled. 'We take the fight to them. Do what we've been trained to, infiltrate and execute. We demand enough money to buy ourselves out of this life, new identities and a place to grow old in them.'

'I don't know,' said Mills. 'It don't feel right. We've done some bad stuff in our time but always for the right reasons, haven't we?' He looked at the others. 'Well, haven't we?'

Nobody could answer him.

'You think they'll go for it?' Mulroney asked later.

'I don't know,' Gleason admitted, opening two bottles of beer and passing one to Mulroney. 'Shaeffer's not thinking straight, and Mills has principles.'

'He'll learn,' said Mulroney taking a sip of his beer. 'Ellroy and Leonard will be OK. They do as their told.'

'And you?'

Mulroney smiled. 'Don't give me that, you know better. How long have we known each other?'

Gleason had to think for a moment. 'Seventeen years.'

'Damn right, two turns in the Gulf and several lifetimes between. We know how it is. This life ain't ever going to change unless we do the changing.' Mulroney shrugged. 'You know I've had plans.'

Gleason nodded and took a long draft of his beer.

'Only an idiot wouldn't think ahead.' Mulroney continued. 'Otherwise we keep at this until *we're* the ones left behind in the desert, or the jungle, or the swamp. Either we die in a foreign land or we get our legs blown off by a mine and put a bullet in our *own* heads cos we just can't stand to sit still. Unless...'

'Unless?'

'Unless we take an opportunity like this.' Mulroney moved closer to Gleason. 'And let's have no more about this being a battlefield crisis of conscience – you wanted that shipment before you even stepped on the boat.'

Gleason stared at him, and Mulroney saw the very worst of both of them in his eyes. Then the older man smiled. For a moment, regardless of their shared history, Gleason had considered killing Mulroney, and Mulroney knew it.

'You think I disagree? If I did we wouldn't be having this conversation.'

'OK.' Gleason nodded. 'I thought about it when the orders came through.'

'Of course you did. But I agree we keep that to

ourselves. These kids don't know the world like we do they're not as...'

'Pragmatic?'

'A nicer word than I was going to use.'

'Then let's stick to it.'

'They need to justify this to themselves, they still want a flag to march under.'

Gleason finished his beer. 'I used to think that way.'

'You and me both, Colonel,' said Mulroney. 'Then we grew up.'

Shaeffer said he needed fresh air, and Gleason had let him go. Shaeffer knew the casual attitude wouldn't last. Gleason would cut them a little slack now as long as they agreed to be pulled back in later.

Shaeffer walked through the long grass, heading away from the house. He walked slowly, smoking a cigarette and glancing around like he was admiring the view. Always mindful of what he would look like if someone was watching him from the house. Just a guy chilling out. Nothing to worry about.

He cut a diagonal across the undergrowth, aiming for the ruins of a gazebo in the far corner. Once upon a time a band would have played here, he guessed, blowing swing and dance tunes to the wealthy owners of the house and their friends.

He stared at it for a moment, looking at the lopsided pillars that supported the roof, the heavy undergrowth that had woven its way between them. He kept his back to the house. Playacting casual interest. *Hey, look at this old place... It must have been great in the old days...*

Then he stepped inside, slowly moved past the plant life and turned to see if he was blocked from view. He was. Keeping an eye on the house through a tiny gap in the branches, he pulled the phone out of his pocket. Glancing down, he saw the screen still showed the address book. He pressed Penelope's name and watched the screen shift to call mode. *Connecting*, it said, a flowing blue arrow illustrating his signal swooping out over the world and changing his life for ever.

'Hello?' came a quiet voice from his hand and he lifted it to his ear in a panic, as much to silence it as answer it. 'Who is this?'

'It's... a friend of Oscar's.'

'A friend? I know Oscar's friends, who is this?'

'I work with Oscar, you know...' He had no idea what to say, no idea how much Oscar would ever have told her. 'It doesn't matter, I just wanted to tell you. There's been an accident. Oscar...'

'Oscar's dead, I know.'

Shaeffer sagged with relief, she already knew! But how could she?

'How did you...?'

'His body was found embedded in the nose of a jumbo jet that crashed in the Gulf of Mexico. News like that travels. Now who is this?'

A jumbo...? Shaeffer couldn't even begin to get his head around that. He nearly hung up. Then his sense of self-preservation kicked in. He tried to decide what to say, peering again at the house through the branches. 'Look,' he said, adopting a more businesslike tone, 'we're all up to our necks out here, our commanding officer's gone…' He had been about to say mad but that was far from true – Gleason knew exactly what he was doing. 'There's a situation here,' he continued, 'and I want out, but my life won't be worth squat unless I'm careful.'

Slowly but surely he began to lay out a deal.

Four

'OK,' said Rex. 'So this guy wants out. Why's it my business?'

'Penelope reported the call,' Esther replied. 'Passed on the details, and within half an hour they're all off the system.'

'What do you mean "off the system"?'

'Just that. None of that S.O.G. team exist on record and there's no detail of an operation to retrieve them. As far as the Company's concerned, they don't exist.'

'More likely their extraction is so sensitive it's off the record.'

'There's no such thing as "off the record" if you dig hard enough. What if Gleason isn't the only one who's gone rogue?'

'You're saying someone's covering his tracks? Burying the data trail?'

'Exactly, leaving him free to get on with whatever the hell he's planning.'

'Why me?'

'Huh?'

'Why not just report it? Make it someone else's problem?'

'Because according to Shaeffer they're in Cuba and you're only a stone's throw away. And because I trust you, and Penelope's good, she deserves someone trustworthy.' She paused, unsure for a moment whether she should continue. Then, with a deep breath: 'And, sorry, but because you've made such a mess of things there you need to vanish and repair your previously gleaming reputation with some acts of unbelievable heroism.'

'I hate you, Esther, you know that, right?'

'Penelope Lupé?' said the old man on Penelope's doorstep. He removed his hat with a gloved hand and doffed it at her. Then, not waiting for the answer, as, in truth, he already knew: 'I'm sorry to disturb you. It's about your husband. May I come in?'

She stepped back to let him past, it never occurring to her to do anything else. It was only as she closed her apartment door that she wondered why she had been so careless. It wasn't in her nature. After all, her husband hadn't been the only one whose monthly wage was paid by the security services.

'Can I see some ID?' she asked, better late than never.

'Of course you may, my dear,' he replied. 'What sort would you prefer?' He reached into his suit jacket and pulled out a black leather wallet. 'I don't have a driver's licence, I'm afraid, I've never been comfortable behind the wheel of a car.' He flipped the wallet open to show a selection of clear plastic folders. 'But I have my social security card.' He passed it to her. 'My pensioner concession card, so useful on the buses.' Again, he handed it over. 'Even a library card.'

'How about something that shows me who you work for?' Penelope asked looking up from the cards in time to see the syringe the old man was thrusting towards her. She turned to avoid it, but he was surprisingly quick, stepping around her, jabbing the needle into her neck and depressing the plunger.

She caught him a slight blow to the side of his head as she turned to face him, her legs buckling underneath her before she could press the attack home.

'Clumsy of me,' the old man said, rubbing at his temple. 'I must remember I'm not as young as I once was.' He moved over towards the couch and sat down. 'Forgive me while I get my breath back.'

Penelope twitched on the polished floorboards of her apartment, her feet rucking up a Mexican rug and knocking over a small occasional table.

'Do try to be careful,' said Mr Wynter. 'I shall have to tidy up before I leave. You wouldn't want an old man to struggle, would you?'

Penelope's face reddened, the tendons in her neck sticking out, teeth clenching together and snipping off the tip of her tongue. The little pink sliver of meat stuck to her chin.

'That's the way, my dear,' Mr Wynter said, leaning back on the rather comfortable couch. 'It could have been worse – in my youth I was known to play awhile. These days I just don't have the energy.'

Penelope gave one last spasm then died, her forehead banging off the floor loud enough that it was followed a few seconds later by a remonstrative tap from below.

'Such delicate neighbours you have,' said Mr Wynter, getting to his feet and moving around the apartment. 'Don't worry, I shall be quiet. I wouldn't want to give you a bad name.'

He moved into the kitchen, opened a few cupboards and then smiled when his eyes fell on an open packet of cookies. 'I do believe in being naughty once in a while,' he said, untwisting the plastic packaging and pushing up a few cookies with his gloved thumb. He pulled one out and popped it in his mouth. Delicious.

Coming back out of the kitchen, he looked around the room for Penelope's cell. It was on a small table in the hall, along with her car keys and purse. He dropped the phone into his jacket pocket and unpacked the purse onto the table. Money, bits of tissue, make-up, all the usual detritus. Nothing troublesome. He replaced everything and put the purse back where he had found it.

He walked through the main living area to the bedroom and en-suite bathroom. By the side of the bed he found a scrap of paper where Penelope had written a phone message. It said 'Shaeffer – Havana – Extraction/ID – Gleason – experimental tech'. That last was ringed with an incredulous question mark next to it. Mr Wynter crumpled the piece of paper and put it in his pocket. Elsewhere looked clean enough. He hadn't expected a distinct paper trail, but it paid to be sure.

He made a call on his cell. 'Hello,' he said. I'd like to book your next available flight from Washington to Nassau please... Yes, Nassau in the Bahamas... Why yes,' he laughed. 'I am a very lucky man, but if you can't enjoy yourself at my age, what's the point?'

Rex had a night to kill before his plane. The time passed slowly. Not only because he was impatient to leave, but also because he was having to spend the time with Ted Loomis, and the man was reluctant to let Rex get off lightly with the day's events.

'"Just observe",' he said as they sat in their hotel bar. 'That should be the main thing they teach people in training.'

'Yeah, right,' said Rex sipping at his beer and not really listening. 'Observe.'

'People always want to jump in,' Ted continued, 'make a name for themselves, be the hero.'

'They do.'

'Not me, I'm happy in my work, a cog in the big machine.'

'Good,' Rex replied. 'Glad you're happy.'

'Not just happy,' said Ted, raising his voice, 'but proud. What we do is important, it keeps people safe!'

'And is often top secret and shouldn't be shouted about in bars,' said Rex.

Ted, realising he was being indiscreet, dropped

his volume. 'Yeah, cos you're Mr Frigging Discreet aren't you? In the van for a couple of minutes, and an operation I have given hours to is flushed down the pan because you couldn't sit still.'

Rex placed his beer carefully on the surface of the bar. He felt it was for the best – if the bottle stayed in his hand he might be tempted to break it on Ted's face, and that wouldn't be good. 'Your case was flushed down the pan because you chose a flaky pervert as a potential asset.'

'Oh grow up and read your history books,' said Ted. 'The CIA doesn't care what people like Dmitri get up to in their spare time. Fact is, if the guy has unusual tastes then all to the better. Something to hold over him.'

'So if you had been in my shoes, you would have been punching the air?'

'Certainly not the asset.'

Rex got to his feet.

'Where the hell are you going?' asked Ted.

Rex leaned in close and whispered in his ear. 'Somewhere I won't end up beating someone to death.'

He walked out of the bar, loud calypso music leaking from pretty much everywhere he walked past as he tried to calm down. Eventually his breathing slowed and his fists unclenched. It's hard to be furious when people keep banging on steel drums; even if you hate that sort of thing, it's the aural equivalent of a Tom and Jerry cartoon and not built for raging through.

He took an outside table at one of the small restaurants and ordered some cracked conch. If he had to spend another night here, his arteries might as well suffer along with the rest of him.

While he ate the deep-fried shell fish, he thought about Shaeffer's phone call. The man had claimed they were in possession of experimental technology. Experimental? The Brits? What had they ever invented except sarcastic sitcoms and bowler hats? More likely it was stolen from another power and sold on to bolster the coffers. After all, you only had to pick up a newspaper to know that the British government had convinced everyone it was desperate for cash. They sounded just like the Republicans, anything to cut public healthcare down to a sticking plaster and a pat on the back. Rex was far from convinced that his presence would be wanted – or needed – but he'd play it carefully, observe from a distance (and wouldn't that please Loomis?) to ensure he wasn't about to get in the way of a sanctioned extraction. If anyone complained – and didn't they always? – he'd blame it on Esther and play nice with the Section Chiefs for a while before they sent him back here. Whether he was needed or not, it would make a welcome palate cleanser from narcotics, you could only work these cases for so long before you felt so damn dirty you needed to take some holiday allowance to shower for a few days.

He returned to his hotel, noticing Ted was still sat on his own in the bar. For a moment, he thought about going over to join him, maybe build a few bridges. Then he was honest with himself about how long it would be before they started a brawl and headed straight to bed.

In the morning, he left the hotel early, skipping breakfast – and therefore any risk of bumping into Ted – and got a cab straight to the airport.

At the check-in desk he took his boarding pass – Business Class, go Esther – and went to wait for his flight.

Mr Wynter tipped back his seat and allowed himself to doze. It was an indulgence, like syrup on oatmeal or a stolen cookie. Better to sleep now than when he arrived. Once in Cuba he would be a busy man.

He had flown from Washington to Nassau then from there to Havana, still the preferred method of circumnavigating US Customs when travelling to Cuba. It was laughable that he of all people was sneaking past the 'powers that be', but he liked to keep a low profile. Besides, it meant he could get a look at Mr Matheson.

Mr Wynter opened his eyes and squinted along the gangway at the man several rows in front of him. He watched as Matheson checked his watch, leaned forward, looked out of the window, picked up the inflight magazine, dumped it back in the seat pouch in front of him and checked the time once more. All of this in the space of a few minutes. Rex Matheson is not a man who likes to sit still, thought Mr Wynter. He is a man that wants the world to move at the same speed as himself. Mr Wynter smiled. We're all young once.

Mr Wynter had no problem waiting. There'd been a time when he might have thought he could push this plane faster by will alone, but no more.

Now he was happy to control what he could – which was considerable – and let the rest get by at its own speed.

'There'll be action soon, Mr Matheson,' he mumbled, slipping contentedly into sleep. 'Have no fear.'

A couple of hours later, Rex walked out of José Martí International and over to one of the small hire car offices adjoining the car park.

'*Dígame, señor*,' said the girl behind the counter, pushing her face into the breeze of a desk fan.

'You have a car booked,' said Rex, 'in the name of Reynolds.'

'The American!' the girl said. 'Who sneaks here from Nassau, yes?'

'Journalist,' said Rex, 'on business.'

'Oh yes, we get a lot of journalists here. They smoke a lot of our cigars and drink a lot of our rum.'

'Not this one.'

'They all say that, too.' She gave him a set of keys. 'Bay number five.'

'*Gracias*, and compliments on your customer service.'

'We aim to please.'

'You missed.'

In bay five, Rex found himself face to face with a car so small he assumed he was supposed to sit on the roof. 'Journalists don't travel in style,' he said, unlocking the door and pushing the driver's seat back as far as it would go.

He drove into Havana, an adventure in itself.

He had no idea how so many old cars were still on the road. The way the locals drove they should have been trashed years ago.

Esther had booked him a room in the old town. This would have been fine, but he wasn't allowed to drive even this toy of a car through some of its streets. Abandoning the car a short walk away (part of him thinking, and hoping, he'd never see it again) he walked the final stretch.

The hotel was a converted colonial house, white walls and black, wrought-iron railings. It was built around a central courtyard, thick curtains of ivy hanging from the balustrades above. The place felt like the revolution had never happened. Rex hoped the plumbing wasn't so nostalgic. He checked in and made his way to his room in the upper far corner of the building. It was huge and empty with two windows in it. One looked down into the central courtyard and the other onto an alley filled with garbage dumpsters. Nice. The sweet smell of what looked like weeks' worth of build-up wafted up along with a few deliriously happy flies.

He closed the window and stretched out on the bed. A soft puff of mouldy air sprang up from the mattress beneath him. He could tell this was going to be a great couple of days.

Mr Wynter watched Rex get into his hire car and drive away from the airport. He went into the hire office.

'Hello there,' he said in perfect Spanish. 'My son was just in here picking up the car.'

'The journalist?' The woman behind the desk asked. 'Your son?'

'Ah, well,' Mr Wynter laughed. 'Son-in-law.'

The woman smiled. 'I thought you looked a bit pale!'

They both laughed at this bit of inane wit. Mr Wynter was in no great rush to hurry her along – the less you seemed to push people, the more they filled the space you left them.

'He did not enjoy his flight I think,' the woman said after a moment. 'He was a little rude.'

Mr Wynter looked mortified. 'I'm so sorry, you must forgive him, he doesn't travel well. And truth be told,' he leaned over the counter as if passing on a little secret, 'I don't think he likes me coming with him on his work trips. But you know, I just love it here and would hate to miss it.'

'Well,' she said, 'at least someone in the family knows how to be nice.'

Mr Wynter winked at her. 'You're too kind. Hey, the thing is, he meant to ask for some directions but you know what these young men are like.'

'They don't like to ask a woman?'

'You've got it.'

She laughed, pulled out Rex's hire contract, and checked the local address given with the booking. 'It's in the old town,' she said. 'Calle de los Oficios. I'll draw you a map.'

'So kind!' Mr Wynter smiled adoringly at her as she scribbled an illegible doodle on a scrap of paper and handed it to him.

'Anything else I can do for you?' she asked.

'Ah...' said Mr Wynter with a shrug. 'If I was

forty years younger...'

They both laughed again, the woman particularly loudly. Mr Wynter blew her a kiss and left the office.

He walked over to the taxi rank, threw his holdall in the back of the first car in line and told the driver to head to the Hostal Moraira on Calle de los Oficios.

As the cab made its way into Havana, Mr Wynter took out his small notebook and jotted down a list of the CIA's affiliated safe-houses in the area. He also tried to bring to mind his memories of the city. Havana had been where he had started his covert life, a young man fresh from school and eager to help his country fight the communist menace.

As a rule, he tried to avoid nostalgia in his work. A man had to exist in the now to be effective. Still, in the old days the information that had led Esther Drummond and thereby Rex Matheson here would never have been exposed. Things were so open now. So many different departments, so much chatter. It had been better when information was a thing you typed onto paper or recorded onto fat coils of magnetic tape. All it took then to make facts disappear was a box of matches and a loose set of morals. Now, thanks to this airborne virus of data transfer and cellphone calls, a man had a mountain of work to keep things dark.

One day, he mused, it would all be a bit much for a man of his age.

One day.

Five

Shaeffer was trapped in the house. As he had expected, Gleason was once again tightening his hold. They'd had their window of false freedom, now they were in lockdown while Gleason and Mulroney worked through the packing crates and began to hatch plans. They worked in the house's wine cellar. The spacious brick chambers were perfect, not only because they kept them safe from prying eyes, but also because the entrance could be locked.

In the last couple of days, the unit had sat on their bedrolls, playing cards or listening to the radio, going slowly mad with boredom as they waited for whatever came next. In a way, Shaeffer guessed, this was all part of the plan. By the time Gleason announced what they were going to do, they would be so desperate to move they'd agree to anything.

Shaeffer had tried to occupy himself by exploring the house. According to Gleason, it had been an unofficial CIA house back in the 1950s and 1960s;

somewhere where things could be conducted off the record. Shaeffer found dark brown stains on the floorboards in one of the bedrooms and an ancient yellow lump that he could have sworn was a tooth. Espionage was a dirty business.

A couple of times he had tried to work his way into the cellar, only too aware that the more he knew about Gleason and Mulroney's plans the more information he would have to trade when the CIA came to pick him up. If I ever get far enough away from this place to make the call, he thought.

It never worked. Even though he had made a great show of enthusiasm for Gleason's hopes for the future, the two older men clearly didn't trust him. They worked down there alone. Sometimes the rest of the platoon would hear weird noises, the buzz of electronics, the soft crump of gunfire. Mostly all was silent.

Shaeffer knew that time was short. Gleason wouldn't want to stay in the same place too long. He wasn't to know that Shaeffer had partially leaked their location. Only partially – Shaeffer wasn't dumb. He had kept the battery on the phone disconnected since making the original call, and there was no way it could be traced unless he switched it on. He wasn't going to do that until he was safely out of the way and in a position to cut a deal.

Once they were on the move, things would be even more difficult. If he was going to make a break for it, he had to do it soon.

*

In the cellar, Gleason ran his finger down the itinerary as Mulroney walked along the neat row of unpacked items. They had rigged up a string of petrol lamps that banished most of the shadows. Neither could altogether believe the claims stacked against many of the items, and they were reluctant to try them out without a secure test site.

'Some of this must be garbage,' said Mulroney. 'I mean just look at the names... A Yeti sidearm... That's Big Foot's revolver, is it? Or this...' He picked up a silver disc, about the size of his palm and looked over Gleason's shoulder at the list. 'Item 9LLL: "hand weapon of aquatic earth reptile". They're making this up.'

'I don't think so,' said Gleason. 'We know some of it works, and the Brits must have known it'd all be tested.'

Mulroney shrugged. 'I guess. Makes you think, though, doesn't it? I mean, we're the people that work beneath the surface, we're the ones that keep the secrets.'

'There are always more secrets.'

'No kidding.'

'But not secret for long.' Gleason picked up the rifle that had made Oscar Lupé vanish.

Mulroney stepped back. 'Hey, if you're going to play with that, maybe I'll leave you to it.'

Gleason ignored him, turning over the rifle in his hands, keeping the barrel facing away from them. The metal was dull and corroded as if it had spent a good deal of time underwater. The shellfish and seaweed certainly suggested as much. Closer inspection showed that the organic elements were not growing on top of the original weapon but were an intrinsic part of it. The thick, grey fronds of weed flowed from the metal with no discernible join. When Shaeffer had tugged on these, the weapon had been triggered. Gleason was careful not to repeat the younger man's mistake.

The paperwork classed it as an 'Ytraxorian Reality Gun'. Most of the items had notes detailing their operation and tested destructive capability. This one simply read: 'Unreliable, appears to shift target's location in space/time, practical military application limited due to fluctuating controls.' Gleason wasn't sure he agreed. 'Shift target's location in space/time'? That seemed interesting indeed. He cast his mind back over the missions he and his unit had carried out, moments when the ability to remove someone (or something?) from the consideration of battle would have been a miracle.

Gleason ran his hands along the surface of the weapon, caressing it. There was a numb, pins and needles sensation on his skin as it touched the weed fronds. Perhaps they conducted electricity? Jesus... perhaps they conducted radiation? He could be brewing up cancers that would kill him in a few months.

'Is it...?' Mulroney came a little closer. 'It *is*... It's *glowing*.'

'Turn down the lamps,' said Gleason. 'Let's see it properly.'

Mulroney did as he was told, and Gleason was lit by a luminescence coming from inside the gun itself.

'This is not good...' said Mulroney.

Gleason thought he might well be right. He squatted down to place the gun on the floor before realising he couldn't let go of it.

'It's got a hold of me,' he said. 'That weed stuff's wrapping round my wrist.'

Mulroney went back to the lamps and turned them back up. 'I'll cut you loose,' he said, pulling a knife from his belt.

'Wait,' said Gleason. 'For all we know, cutting into it will trigger the damn thing. I don't think it means harm.'

'You're talking like it's alive.'

'Yeah,' said Gleason. 'I am. I think it is.'

In fact he *knew* it was, but didn't know how to express the fact. Not without sounding ridiculous. That same tingling he had felt on his hands now extended up his arms and towards his head. Like the creep of an anaesthetic injected through the back of the hand. When the sensation reached his head, fizzing at the base of his skull, it was impressions that flooded through him rather than unconsciousness. It was nothing so precise as communication. He couldn't say that the rifle was talking to him. Still, he began to understand. He began to *know*.

Two years earlier...

'That can't be comfortable,' said Jack Harkness, switching off the deep-fat fryer and helping the gelatinous creature to extricate its head from the submerged basket.

As it fell back onto the dirty floor tiles, it sighed with relief, though the noise that came out resembled a child imitating a motorcycle. This was probably because its lips had melted together, bloated purple slugs that dribbled onto its cheeks and formed a cat's cradle over its black teeth like hot mozzarella.

'Something tells me the safety buffers on your transmat are playing up,' said Jack. 'You really shouldn't be hopping around the universe with faulty tech like that. You're lucky you didn't end up hanging out of a wall.'

'Lucky?' Gwen asked, looking at the state of the creature's face.

Jack held his finger to his lips and walked over to her. 'For all we know it was born that ugly,' he whispered. 'Now go help Ianto clear up out front.'

'Ianto doesn't need my help,' Gwen scowled. 'He's perfectly capable of managing on his own.'

'Keeping people out of Kool Fried Chicken late on a Saturday night?' asked Jack. 'Have you seen the streets out there? I give him five minutes before he's bottled by a fat drunk or has his clothes bitten off by a Hen party. It'll take both of you. With guns.'

Gwen sighed and headed out of the kitchen.

Jack looked closer at the creature, trying to define where hard shell and soft flesh began and ended. It looked like a turtle that had been roughly chopped then sculpted back together again. Perhaps that was also the fault of a faulty transmat?

Next to the body was a weapon of some sort, a long rifle festooned with organic elements. He nudged it to one side in case its owner should decide to turn nasty. He pulled a medical scanner out of his pocket and swept it over the creature's body. He glanced at the numbers and gave a little mental shrug before turning the screen towards the creature. 'You'll have a better idea than me how you're doing,' he said. 'Can't say I've ever met your species before and, believe me, that's a rarity.'

The creature gurgled, raised its hands and clapped the palms together.

'Hang on,' said Jack, tapping at the controls on his earpiece until he could understand what the creature was trying to say.

'...lanet Ytraxor,' it said in a surprisingly mellifluous tone, not dissimilar to Michael

Hordern. 'Am dying, can feel the wilting in my lung nodes.'

'Never good,' said Jack scratching his chin in some bemusement.

'Must give last song,' it continued. 'Will you hear?'

'As long as it's not "Angels", you have my full attention.'

Jack had been expecting a further round of guttural plosives and hand waving – a functional language for a species used to spending time in the water, he guessed. Instead, the creature opened its mouth as wide as it could and began to sing. It was a noise somewhere between bird and whale song, a low bass drone combined with complex trills of immense range. There was more to the noise than music. Contained within the sounds were images and impressions that flooded Jack's mind so quickly he had to support himself against the wall. The species had an even more impressive method of communication, he realised, sitting down on the sticky tiles and closing his eyes to focus on the information the song relayed. It was a download of images and scenes, a compressed package of events channelled directly into the brain where it could slowly unpack and display itself to the recipient.

He saw Ytraxor, as if from above, a mass of ice, a planet slowly freezing as its sun grew cold. He saw its people, once ocean dwellers, now huddled in caves, avoiding the encroaching glaciers and fighting over the diminishing space that was left. Some of the creatures were, like the specimen before him, bulky and armoured, others taller and thinner wearing light robes. This was a caste system, Jack realised, a race genetically engineered for their role in life: the warriors and the elite. He saw a third Ytraxorian, thin like the elite but with gleaming, non-organic elements built into their flesh. These were the scientists he understood, the technicians, the thinkers.

One of these technicians was holding up a rifle, much like the one this creature had carried, showing it to one of the Ytraxorian elite.

The two of them began to talk and, though the barking and gestures meant nothing to Jack, their meaning seeped into his head along with the images.

'What's this?' asked the elite.

'A weapon, sire,' the technician replied, 'bred by the time-travel research team.'

The elite – ArchDuke, thought Jack, they think of him as the ArchDuke – tilted its head on one side in a manner that Jack understood to be sceptical. 'What does it do?' it asked.

'Removes its target from its current position in space/time and sends it elsewhere.'

'Really?' the ArchDuke replied. 'If we can do that then why don't we just shoot ourselves back a few thousand years, before the ice?'

'Ytraxorian tissue still isn't stable when exposed to Chronon radiation, sire,' the technician replied, and Jack suddenly experienced a mental picture of an Ytraxorian technician exploding as the rifle's beam was turned on it, showering the lab in guts, sucker and fin. 'Also there is a question of aim.'

'Aim?'

'While it's possible to control the degree of time shift, the physical location is hard to fix. Put simply the target could end up anywhere, and the odds of them arriving somewhere safe, not way above our heads or embedded in the rock beneath our feet, are impossible to predict. Of course when using it as a weapon…'

'Who cares?'

'Precisely. It can also project a far weaker beam that temporally alters the matter it's aimed at.'

'Temporally alters?'

'Ages or rejuvenates it, sire.'

'I could shoot myself with it and have the body of a podling?'

'You could, sire, but considering the likely life span of our planet, I wouldn't recommend it. What would be the point?'

'So it's just a vicious bastard of a gun then, really?'

'A very vicious bastard, sire, yes. Programmed as always, with the appropriate Honour Filters.'

'Oh yes, heaven forbid we should kill in cold blood.'

The concept of honour filters circled around Jack's head for a moment before coalescing in a concept he understood. The Ytraxorians, once a proud feudal race, believed that the burgeoning potential of technology shouldn't entirely rob the battlefield of skill. All weaponry came preloaded with software that graded the payload according to the bloodthirsty intent of the Ytraxorian holding it. A soldier on an Ytraxorian battlefield couldn't just pull the trigger. He had to be *really good* at pulling the trigger.

'Ytraxorians are crazy,' said Jack. 'It's a wonder you have a planet left.'

And then the dying alien's song built in volume, and Jack flinched as the image of Ytraxor burning filled his head. Line after line of Ytraxorians marched on rival factions, the air filling with the dull throb of rifle fire as the population swiftly eradicated itself.

'Oh God...' Jack cried, the roar of battle so loud in his head he could swear the tiles beneath him were rattling themselves loose.

In no time, there were only two Ytraxorians left, facing one another across the battle-ravaged cavern of their long-dead ruling elite.

'Look,' said one of them, the Ytraxorian that was now singing to him, Jack realised. 'Maybe this has gone a bit far.'

'Arrgghh!' screamed the other and shot his fellow being so hard and so successfully that it ended up several parsecs away in Cardiff, its head in a dirty deep-fat fryer in the sort of nasty fast-food dive you needed to be drunk to eat from. All things considered, a good shot.

The song finished. The creature died.

Jack looked at the rifle that had, indirectly, caused the death of its owner. After taking a moment to get his thoughts together, he got to his feet and picked it up. A light electric charge passed through his fingers and the fronds of seaweed appeared to writhe of their own volition, reaching for his fingers.

He let it grasp him, felt it communicating with him just as its dying owner had, connecting directly with his brain and making him understand what it was that he held in his hands. The power it represented was chilling. He tore his hands free and wedged the gun beneath his arm so that it wasn't in contact with his skin.

He looked at the creature on the floor, bubbling and popping as its flesh began to lose cohesion. Whether it was natural for an Ytraxorian upon death or a delayed reaction to the effect of being blasted so far across time and space, Jack couldn't tell.

He stuck his head around the serving hatch and grinned at Ianto and Gwen as they wrestled a 'glandular' lady in a plastic tiara back out of the doors and away from her precious buckets of fried bird. 'Having fun?' he asked, then chuckled at the expressive hand gestures they offered.

'I have bruises,' said Ianto, 'on places that have never been bruised in the line of duty before.'

'That rather depends on what you consider your duty,' said Jack, kissing him on the cheek and waving at the large lady now stuck on the outside of the glass.

'Never eat something that comes in a bucket!' he shouted to her.

'And he's not talking about chicken,' Ianto added.

'Gentlemen, please,' said Gwen. 'Have you finished back there or what?'

'Nearly,' said Jack. 'Don't suppose either have you have seen a mop?'

Six

Mr Wynter sat in the shade of a bougainvillea bush in the central courtyard of the Hostal Moraira. He ordered a coffee which arrived just as Rex appeared on the upper balcony, having changed into a short-sleeved shirt and a pair of jeans. First you'll go to the docks, thought Mr Wynter, because you know they arrived by boat and someone must remember them hiring transport to ferry several packing crates as well as themselves. It was a logical first step but not one that Mr Wynter felt it necessary to duplicate. After all, he already had a good idea of where Gleason and company would be.

Once upon a time, the CIA had had a reasonable presence in Cuba. These days they preferred to concentrate efforts elsewhere and leave it to border control. Gleason had come here because it was close but also because he knew somewhere here that would suit their purpose as a temporary base. He knew somewhere big and empty enough to accommodate a handful of men and their cargo. Somewhere that was secluded so that their business would go unregarded. Somewhere that had never appeared on any official CIA paperwork – Gleason wasn't to know that his presence in Havana was compromised, but he still wouldn't turn up at an active CIA residence, the man was a professional. *Was* being the operative term, Mr Wynter thought, sipping his coffee. Now Gleason was just a dead man walking.

Mr Wynter knew of a place that fitted all the necessary requirements and a glance at Gleason's operation history suggested he might know of it too.

Finishing his coffee, Mr Wynter went to reception and booked a room.

He dropped his holdall on the bed inside and then left the building, working his way through the streets of old Havana in search of the right sort of bar. Eventually he settled on a small place called Club Excalibur at the end of a gloomy side street. Why it deemed itself worthy of such mythological grandeur was not obvious. As Mr Wynter entered the building, he had to wave his hands in front of his face to dispel enough cigar smoke to see. The clientele was predictably questionable. Anyone found enjoying an early-afternoon drink in a dark, cancerous lung of a place like this was bound to be a member of the gutterati.

Mr Wynter pulled up a stool at the bar and ordered a Daiquiri Natural.

He was approached before the barman could even begin making his drink. Possibly this was a gentleman's agreement so the establishment didn't waste rum on customers that would soon be too dead to drink it.

'You are American,' said the voice at his shoulder.

'Is that a question or are you just showing off?' Mr Wynter turned around and smiled at the large Cuban behind him. The man looked to have been built from butcher's offcuts. His face was lumpen with scar tissue and, when he smiled, he showed Mr Wynter little but gums. 'You look perfect,' Mr Wynter said.

'Your eyesight must be bad for you to come in here in the first place,' said the Cuban, 'but you must be completely blind if you like my face. Maybe I'll give you one to match?'

'Then you wouldn't earn all the money I plan on paying you for a few jobs I'd like taking care of,' Mr Wynter replied. 'Which seems a shame really.' He turned to the barman. 'Where's my drink?' he asked. 'I haven't got all day.' The barman, looking somewhat surprised, turned away and began mixing.

'What jobs?' asked the Cuban.

'Oh, you know,' said Mr Wynter. 'All the usual stuff – driving me around, sharing your local knowledge, beating people up.'

'I'm good at that,' the Cuban replied, offering another gummy smile.

'I just bet you are,' said Mr Wynter.

Rex moved through the busy harbour until he found a relatively quiet spot. Sitting down on a coil of rope, he called Esther.

'Hey,' she said. 'You found anything yet?'

'Patience, woman,' he replied. 'I only just got here.'

'Sorry,' Esther replied 'I'm just...'

'What is it?' asked Rex.

'Penelope Lupé was found dead in her apartment.'

'Dead how?'

'Heart attack, apparently.'

'Apparently?'

'Well, what do you think?'

'I think that if Gleason and his unit are here in Cuba but someone's killing people that are connected, then you should keep your mouth shut, especially on an open line.'

'Sorry.'

'It's OK. Don't worry, I'm on this, and I'll find out who killed her. For now I need you focused, yes?'

'Of course.' A slight pause as she tried to put a little more steel in her voice. 'I'm fine.'

'Damn right you are. Now... first problem: he's going to call her, so... we have her cell?'

'No, and guess what, according to company records she never had one. They are tidying this up so tight...'

'Tight enough I can't believe S.O.G.'s not involved. Seriously, Esther, this stinks worse by the minute.'

'I know. Sorry. There is one piece of good news: I cleared things with Broderick. You have sanction in this until someone from higher up slaps his wrists.'

'Broderick actually approved this?'

'I know. I think it's because he's always had the hots for me.'

'Not that he really likes and respects my work?'

'He hates you, Rex.'

'Can't think why.'

'You refused to hand over the route mapping in Venezuela.'

'I suggested he would be better not interfering and let me get on with my job. I was perfectly friendly.'

'You told him to suck your balls.'

'The very definition of friendly. I don't let just anyone suck them.'

'He didn't take it that way.'

'His loss, they're nice balls. Succulent.'

'I'm hanging up on you now.'

'I told you to do that five minutes ago.'

The phone went dead in his ear.

Rex got up and made his way towards where a collection of men were hauling crates onto the quayside.

'Hey,' he called. 'Where can I hire a truck?'

They looked at him as if he was speaking Dutch.

'My Spanish isn't that bad,' he said. 'Where can I hire some transport?'

Eventually, one of the men pointed further up the quay and so began a slow game of tag as he worked his way from one group to another until eventually he found himself, by a general consensus of the people working at the harbour, face to face with Juan de Marcos Rodriguez.

Rodriguez was a small man, sat on a tatty deckchair in the far corner of the harbour. He was looking out over the water, scratching at a stained patch on his vest and puffing on the ubiquitous cigar. From the smell of him, it wasn't all he liked to smoke and Rex spotted pinprick burn holes in the fabric of the unbuttoned shirt he wore. Rodriguez, in turn, had Rex pegged as Customs from the off, and no matter how often the agent tried to convince him otherwise he was defensive to all his questions.

'I just want to know if you hired out a truck,' Rex insisted. 'I don't care how much you charged, what checks you made—'

'I didn't break any law,' Rodriguez insisted. 'It's not my business where a boat comes from or what it carries.'

'Of course not,' Rex agreed. 'You just hire out transport. That's OK. I get that.'

'I know, that's what I tell you.'

'So did you?'

'Did I what?'

Rex restrained himself from shooting the man. It was broad daylight and there would be witnesses. 'Did you hire out a truck to some Americans?'

'I might have done, who can say?' said Rodriguez. 'I'd have to check my files.'

Rex sighed and reached for his wallet. He had already loaded up on local currency knowing full well he would have ample opportunity to spend it. He pulled out a couple of notes. 'So check your files.'

Rodriguez pocketed the notes, scratched at his beard and then pulled out a piece of paper from the pocket of his shirt. Rex could see it was an advert for a local nightclub, nothing more. Rodriguez pretended that wasn't the case, scrutinising the paper for a while and then looking back at Rex. 'Yes I did. But I have no idea where they went.'

'You let them drive off with your truck without taking an address? I don't think so.'

'The American man,' Rodriguez smiled, 'had a trustworthy face.'

'And a bigger wallet than mine?' asked Rex.

'Much bigger.'

'How much would it take for you to remember, do you think?'

Rodriguez thought of a number and doubled it.

Rex nodded. 'I could pay that,' he said, 'or I could physically drag you over to the port authority and have them search you for marijuana. How would that work? Still pretty flaky about pot here, aren't they? What would you be looking at, ten years? Twenty maybe, depending on how much is in that pocket you keep rubbing.'

'You wouldn't do that,' said Rodriguez, whipping his hand away from his jeans and suddenly all charm. 'I am just a businessman, doing nobody any harm.'

'My friend,' said Rex, 'I have known you all of a couple of minutes, and I would already beat you to death with that deckchair if it meant I could get the address I want. I am a very driven man.'

'You are a son of a bitch.'

'That too. Now give me the address, or for the next ten years you're going to be eating burned rice with one hand while the other covers your asshole.'

Rodriguez gave him the address.

Mr Wynter's new employee was called Famosa, and he was the proud owner of his very own car. A yellow and green Chevrolet that wore its rust and dented bodywork as proud scars of battle.

'This thing's older than me,' said Mr Wynter as he climbed into the passenger seat.

'It goes forward and back,' said Famosa with a laugh, 'but the exhaust leaks inside so keep your window open, I do not wish to be poisoned.'

Mr Wynter shook his head in disbelief and kept his hand over his mouth as the car pulled out into traffic.

Famosa drove to the edge of the old town, following Mr Wynter's directions. Eventually, they were at the end of the track leading to the Hernandez House.

'Stop here,' said Mr Wynter. 'I want to walk up alone.'

'What's to stop me keeping the money you've given me and driving off?' asked Famosa.

'Greed,' Mr Wynter replied, stepping out of the car and walking along the track.

After a few minutes, he came to the little house belonging to Angelo's grandmother. The boy was sat on the front porch, poking at a gecko lizard with a stick.

'Hello, young man,' said Mr Wynter, his Spanish

accent good enough to hide any hint of his being American. Mr Wynter was the perfect chameleon when he wanted to be. 'I wonder if you'd like to earn a few pesos?'

Rex pulled his little car up at the address Rodriguez had given him and looked out of the window. It was a gap between buildings, the result of old bomb damage at a guess.

Never really doubting it was a waste of time, he got out of the car and walked over. The rubble-covered ground was thick with weeds, grass and trash. Bags of it had been dumped there to cook in the sunshine.

'Maybe the American wasn't that trustworthy after all,' he said. He went back to his car and drove back to the hotel

Mr Wynter stood in Angelo's bedroom and looked out of the window towards the Hernandez House. There was no sign of movement, but the chain on the gates and the tracks in the dirt backed up what the boy had told him. For sure, this was the place. Now all he had to do was form a plan of action.

He looked around Angelo's room for a piece of paper. Eventually he settled for pulling a poster of the footballer Lester Moré from the wall above Angelo's bed and tearing a piece off it. Turning it over to write on the blank reverse, he jotted down the address of Angelo's grandmother's house plus a few general directions. He then folded the piece of paper and dropped it into his waistcoat pocket.

Arriving back at Famosa's car, the Cuban was

resting on the bonnet, taking in the sunshine.

'Come on, my friend,' said Mr Wynter. 'I have just one more job for you to do, and then we can call it a day.'

The Cuban smiled. 'Easy money.'

'Don't be so sure,' said Mr Wynter, patting the Cuban on the back and slipping the piece of paper into the pocket of the man's shirt without his noticing. 'We're at the "beating people up" part of the deal.'

'It's not a problem,' insisted Famosa. 'I told you I'm good at that, didn't I?'

'So you did, so you did,' Mr Wynter replied.

Back at the hotel, Rex ordered a cold drink from the bar and took it straight up to his room. He wanted to cool down and clean up. Maybe, once he felt a bit more human, he'd head back into town and grab some food. Act like a tourist for the rest of the day – there seemed little else he could do right now.

He necked the soda in a couple of long draughts and then went through to the bathroom to check out the shower. After a godawful – and hardly hopeful – groan from the water tank, the water began to flow and Rex was relieved to find it both hot and strong.

He stripped off, climbed into the bath and pulled the shower curtain across.

For a few minutes he just stood there, letting the water gush over his head and down his body. He felt the last couple of days go with it. A sense of calm pouring over him.

The water might be hot for now but only a fool would be optimistic for the long term, so he grabbed the soap and lathered up, scrubbing hard until his skin tingled. He looked around for shampoo and saw nothing.

'Typical,' he sighed, pulling the curtain aside to look across to the sink in the hope of spotting a complimentary bottle there. He came face to face with Famosa, who was stepping through the bathroom door, a stubby pocket knife in his hand. Famosa looked just as startled as Rex, though not for long. He lunged at Rex who jumped sideways to avoid the knife, slipping in the bath and tumbling against the far wall.

He snatched at the shower curtain, twisting it over the extended knife and throwing all his strength at spinning Famosa round so he would have his back to him. Famosa moved more easily than Rex had expected and, as he reached around to put a choke hold on the man, he found out why. Famosa grabbed Rex's arm and threw him over his shoulder. Rex crashed against the bathroom door banging it closed.

'Hey,' called an English voice from next door. 'Keep the noise down, would you? Some of us are having a siesta!'

Lucky old you, Rex thought, rolling towards the sink as Famosa uncurled the shower curtain from his knife hand.

'You should just relax,' said Famosa. 'Let me kill you quickly.'

'Of course I should,' said Rex reaching for the large round shaving mirror hanging above the sink. 'What great advice.' He unhooked the mirror and swung it towards Famosa, who kept backing away, the wind whistling as Rex swept it back and forth. Rex swung the mirror at the knife and managed to knock it from the man's hand. Famosa shrugged, raised his hands in the air and charged at Rex. Rex ducked and thrust the mirror, sideways on, so that the frame jabbed the big Cuban between the legs.

Famosa grunted and twisted to Rex's left. Rex brought the mirror up and smashed it down on the Cuban's head. It shattered, and cut a line in Famosa's forehead that instantly began to bleed.

Famosa swore at Rex, one hand shooting out and punching him in the face. Rex staggered back against the bathroom door, vision blurring and head spinning. He heard, rather than saw, the Cuban charge at him. He stepped to the side and was relieved to hear Famosa's fist burst through the cheap, chipboard panel of the bathroom door. Rex knew he had to keep moving while he had the advantage. He opened the door and swung it back so Famosa was trapped behind it, wedged against the wall. Rex yanked the door and then slammed it again and again at Famosa, whose wedged arm swung around through the hole in the door, bloodied fist opening and closing as he tried to get a grip on Rex.

Rex's feet slipped in water spilling from the still-running shower, and he lost his momentum. Famosa's free hand snatched at the back of his head and pulled it forward to slam against the door. Falling to the floor, Rex just managed to scoot backwards into the bedroom as Famosa yanked his arm out of the hole in the door, crying out as the splintered wood gouged a rut along it.

'Seriously,' came the English voice again, banging on the wall. 'Whatever you're doing in there, I'm sure it's great fun but the rest of the hotel doesn't need to hear it.'

'Great fun,' Rex murmured, getting to his feet and looking around for his gun. Famosa lunged forward, and Rex moved to one side, grabbing the back collar of the man's shirt and using it to yank the man backwards. Famosa fell to the floor with enough of a crash to make a decorative vase on the sideboard jump up in the air and smash on the floor. Rex punched down into Famosa's face as hard as he could, slamming the palm of his hand into the bridge of the man's nose. Not waiting to see if that was enough, he yanked the disorientated man forward, slipped beneath him and twisted his neck around as hard as it would go. There was a low crunch and Rex fell back onto the floor, the now dead Cuban lying on top of him.

'Sorry,' he shouted after a second. 'Slipped in the shower.'

'How many times, for Christ's sake?' asked the neighbour before moaning quietly to himself, the words too low for Rex to hear.

Rex got to his feet and dragged Famosa back into the bathroom. There was a knock on the door.

Rex picked up a piece of broken mirror and checked his face, turning the shower head towards it to wash away some of the blood, before turning off the faucet and walking back through to the bedroom.

'Hello,' called a woman's voice through the door. 'It is the manager, we hear a lot of noise.'

Rex opened the door a crack and stuck his head through. 'I fell in the shower,' he said again. 'Couple of times actually. Everything's fine.'

'Really, sir?' the woman looked down a huge hooked nose at him, clearly not convinced. 'I suppose you wouldn't mind if I took a quick look?'

Rex swung the door wide open and stood there naked in the doorway. 'Kind of a bad time,' he said, as the manager put her hands to her face. 'Maybe a little later? Everything's fine though. I broke the mirror but I'm happy to pay. You want the money now?' He patted his right buttock as if checking for a wallet. 'Oh, right... wrong pair of pants.'

'Later!' the manager said. 'Go and cover yourself! Never have I seen such a thing.' She stormed off.

'Nose like that, I can well believe it,' Rex muttered and stepped back inside.

He went through to the bathroom and crouched next to Famosa's dead body.

'So who were you, then?' Rex asked, rifling through the man's pockets. He pulled out a battered old wallet, stuffed with a good deal of cash. 'Paid you well,' said Rex as he ran his thumb along the notes. There was a driver's licence and ID Card giving the man's name as Eduardo Enrique Famosa.

Rex threw the wallet to one side and checked the rest of the man's pockets. In his shirt there was a piece of paper with an address and some vague directions on it. 'Where you met your employer, maybe?' said Rex, taking the piece of paper through to the bedroom and slipping it into the pocket of his jeans.

He went back into the bathroom, pulled Famosa's body out by his feet and dragged him over to the far window that overlooked the trash. He opened the window and took a quick look: there was nobody around. He hoisted the dead body up, lifting him by his armpits. Famosa's head lolled from side to side on its broken neck. Rex poked the head through the window and then lifted, straining against the dead weight. Slowly he fed the body through the window until, eventually, there was enough weight dangling outside to pull the rest after it. There was a soft crunch as the body bounced off one of the brimming dumpsters and fell behind it.

'Perfect,' said Rex. He closed the window and gathered up the pieces of broken vase from the floor. He took them into the bathroom and dumped them in the sink, adding the pieces of broken mirror. He looked at the door. Not a whole lot he could do about that except claim he'd broken it when he fell. Hell, give the woman enough money and she'd believe whatever he wanted her to.

He got back into the shower and quickly soaped himself off. He was bleeding from a number of places but nothing too major. Once clean, he towelled himself dry and got dressed.

Pulling the piece of paper from his jeans he looked at the address.

Dinner could wait, first he'd see if he had better

luck here than at the address Rodriguez had given him.

Mr Wynter was sitting in the central courtyard again when Rex came out of his room and down the stairs.

The old man had listened to the fight with some amusement. For a moment or two, he had wondered whether Famosa might get the better of Mr Matheson; he had hoped not, naturally, but the noises had gone on long enough for him to be far from sure.

He watched the man walk through to reception where the manager, clearly still incensed with the disturbance, went from red-faced and loud to demure and obsequious as soon as Rex handed over a large roll of banknotes. Probably the money I paid to Famosa, Mr Wynter thought with a smile. So long as it went to a good cause.

He lifted his face into the late-afternoon sun and closed his eyes for a few minutes, enjoying the warmth, letting Mr Matheson have a brief head start. After all, Mr Wynter knew exactly where the man was going.

Seven

All we have to do is learn how to control it, he had said, and wasn't that proving to be a greater battle than he had hoped?

Gleason closed his eyes, felt the tingle of the weed fronds in his hands and tried to find that sense of understanding he had achieved before. He and Mulroney had gathered a selection of test objects from around the house and, one by one, Gleason had made them disappear.

But that had been the limit of their tests. Who knew where the objects had gone? There was no way of knowing whether they had been sent back in time or simply shifted in space. Gleason knew which he had been aiming for, focusing his mind on the desired goal and letting his fingers move amongst the weed fronds in response to his subconscious.

To begin with, that alone had been an almost impossible task; Gleason was not a man who found it easy to relax, certainly not with a gun in his hand. That done – and he was finding it easier each time, relaxing into the firing of the weapon, relaxing into the imagined act of violence – he needed to stretch the weapon's capabilities and his own ability to control them.

Mills couldn't have knocked on the door at a better time.

Corporal Owen Mills had always been a dreamer. He had filled a childhood in Des Moines with Big Plans for the future. These had included all the usual clichés: air pilot, astronaut, cop, football star... Most kids hit a point where, tired of the real world not living up to the Technicolor fantasies, they surrendered to reality. Not Mills. He spent so much of his time dreaming that the real world passed him by.

So, with a below-average education and parents that had long since washed their hands of their fantasist son, he found himself watching the American forces in Iraq and thinking: here's another dream, one I might just be able to achieve. Owen Mills decided he wanted to be a hero.

He enlisted, he trained, he shipped out to Afghanistan.

And, against all expectation, Mills had found something he was good at. He obeyed orders and kept a clear head; he could aim a rifle when the world was falling in around him; and he *survived*. In conflict, that will always be the greatest achievement of all. He developed a solid reputation throughout the ranks, and when Colonel Cotter Gleason found himself a man down and looking for new blood, he found it in Owen Mills.

Gleason had always had his doubts about the boy – and even though he was in his mid-twenties Mills would always be a 'boy' to Gleason – not concerns about his ability to fight, but rather his politics. Mills was an idealist, still chasing that heroic dream. To Gleason that was a bump in the road they were bound to hit some day. He couldn't bring himself to dismiss the boy for his beliefs – how the hell could he? – but he had always known that one day he might have cause to regret them.

Mills, for his part, had done his job within Gleason's unit as well as he had elsewhere. However much he may have clung to his principles, he soon found, like most of us, that it was easy enough to justify almost anything if you looked at it the right way. Mills never stopped dreaming as his finger pulled the trigger.

But this was too much.

He had spent the time since Gleason's announcement sitting on his own at the top of the house trying to rationalise and justify the things his commanding officer was suggesting. He wasn't an idiot, he knew that going against Gleason would almost certainly be a risk to his wellbeing. The Colonel was not a man who accepted not getting what he wanted. Still, he couldn't see another option. He either stood up for himself or became something he couldn't bear to be.

Having worked up his courage, he walked down to the wine cellar and put his ear to the door. He could hear Mulroney and Gleason talking. He took a deep breath, reminded himself why this was something he had to do and then knocked on the door.

After a few seconds, it was opened by Mulroney.

'What do you want, Mills?' he asked. 'We're kind of busy here, you know?'

'I know, sir.' Mills swallowed down his nerves. 'But I need to speak to the Colonel.'

Mulroney stared at him for a moment, trying to read the young man's face. 'You sure about that, Mills?' he asked.

'Quite sure, sir.'

Mulroney nodded and stepped back so that Mills could enter.

Mills walked down the short flight of stone steps, walked up to Gleason and saluted.

Gleason smiled and gave a gentle salute back. 'Why the ceremony, Mills?' he asked. 'You got a proclamation to make?'

'Yes, sir.' Mills loosened slightly. 'Sort of, sir. I've thought about our current situation, and I've decided I can no longer be a part of this unit, sir.'

'Oh, really?' Gleason stepped in close, wanting to see how long it would take to break the kid's confidence. 'Too good for us?'

'I just don't believe in our current course of action, sir,' Mills replied. 'When I enlisted in this army, I did so with a set of beliefs and morals that I have tried to stand by ever since. I believe our current actions to compromise those beliefs. Therefore I cannot continue.'

Gleason nodded and smiled. 'Practise that little speech, Corporal?'

Mills hesitated, not wanting to give a truthful answer and undercut himself.

Gleason shook his head. 'So what are you going to do now?'

'Sir?'

'Well it's all very well making your little speech, drawing your line in the sand, but what's the next step?'

Mills thought for a second. 'I'll leave, sir.'

'You'll leave? You'll just up and stroll out of here, will you? And what will you tell people about us?'

'I will denounce your actions, sir.' Mills realised he was likely damning his own future. 'Though obviously I can't stop you,' he added, 'and if you were gone from here by the time I reported in...'

Gleason laughed. 'That's it? Seriously?' He began to stroll around Mills, circling the young man. 'So basically, you want a free pass? You want to be able to stroll out of here and resume your life as normal. You can't stay with us because we compromise your oh-so-stringent beliefs, but those beliefs aren't strong enough for you to man up and stand by them?'

'Sir?'

'Don't call me "sir", Mills,' said Gleason. 'If you're not willing to follow me, then you shouldn't give me the credit of rank.'

'I just—'

Gleason punched him in the kidneys, and Mills dropped to his knees.

'If your principles are so damned strong, Mills,' Gleason continued, 'you should be willing to fight for them. You shouldn't just walk out of here, you should grow a pair and try and stop me.'

He kicked Mills in the back, sending the young man face-first into the dust of the cellar floor. Mills, realising he had to fight unless he wanted to stay in the dirt, rolled over and got back to his feet, ready to swing a punch. He wasn't fast enough. Gleason got there before him, hitting him on the side of the face and driving him back down to his knees.

'That's better, soldier!' Gleason shouted. 'Fight for what you believe in!'

Mills roared, got to his feet and charged at Gleason, wrapping his arms around the man's midsection and shoving him back against the far wall. The old soldier crashed into a rotting wine rack, and an explosion of dust and wood fragments erupted around him.

Mills stared at Gleason. He couldn't quite believe what he'd just done.

Gleason, still lying on his back, looked up at him and slowly shook his head. 'That's it? One sign of life and then all over?' Slowly he got to his feet. 'Looks like you've learned nothing in this unit, kid,' he said, 'and you only get one free shot.'

Faster than Mills could react, Gleason swung his leg at Mills' knee and there was a sickening crack as the leg folded backwards. Mills screamed as he toppled over, and Gleason aimed another kick at the boys stomach, winding him and silencing the noise.

Gleason looked over to Mulroney. 'Didn't want to help an old man?'

Mulroney smiled. 'Like you needed it, Colonel.'

Gleason looked down at Mills, retching in the dust. 'Looks like we've got ourselves a test subject.'

Shaeffer had heard the shouting coming from the cellar. They all had.

'What the hell's he doing down there?' he said, looking to Leonard and Ellroy.

Leonard shrugged. 'Who knows?'

Mills screamed, and Shaeffer looked at the other two imploringly. 'You just going to sit there?'

'The Colonel can handle it,' said Ellroy.

Shaeffer shook his head. 'So that's it, is it? That's the way you're going to play this now? Screw Mills?'

He ran towards the cellar and then stopped. With Mulroney and Gleason there, alongside several crates of high-end weaponry, there wasn't much he could do. Would it really help Mills if he burst in there and got himself killed? Wasn't it better to take this opportunity to run? The phone was in his pocket – he hadn't dared leave it anywhere in case the others searched his stuff, and it stayed with him even when he slept. What else did he need? His gun. He wasn't going anywhere without that.

He went to the empty room he had been using to sleep in and grabbed his handgun. Standard-issue SIG Sauer P226, he checked the magazine, a full complement of twenty 9mm Parabellum cartridges. Parabellum, he thought, from the Latin 'prepare for war'. Damn right.

He tucked the gun into his jeans and pulled a shirt loose over his T-shirt so that it was covered. He looked over to the other bedroll in the room. It was Mills's.

'Shit,' Shaeffer sighed. 'Shit, shit, shit…'

He left the room, glancing across the hall to make sure Leonard and Ellroy were staying put. They were playing cards, Leonard's back to the door and Ellroy out of sight inside the room. Sloppy boys, thought Shaeffer. I could just stroll in there and shoot the pair of you. Maybe he should. No, this didn't have to go that far, at least not yet. They'd chosen their sides, but maybe they would change their minds once things really got out of hand.

He made his way downstairs, keeping to the edges of the steps and trying to be as silent as possible.

He hesitated in the hallway. The front door was right there, he could be through it and away without anyone knowing. Who knew how much of a head start he could get if he just ran now?

Then there came the renewed sound of Mills in pain. Quieter now, with a pleading tone.

Shaeffer really wished he hadn't heard that.

He walked towards the kitchen and the entrance to the wine cellar, pulling out his gun and gripping it tightly in his hand as he crept closer and closer to the door.

He paused for a second, his hand resting lightly on the handle. From inside there came the low hum of something electronic then a plosive coughing sound. Shaeffer remembered that sound only too well; last time he'd heard it, it had been his hand on the trigger. Opening the door, he pointed his gun down the stairs and slowly descended a couple of steps. A wheezing noise rose up to meet him. It was coming from a patch of darkness between the light thrown from the kitchen behind him and the oil lamps in the cellar below. A no man's land of shadow between two worlds.

'Mills?' Shaeffer shouted, almost ready to bolt and to hell with the young soldier. 'If you're there, then come on, I'll cover you.'

'That you, Shaeffer?' said Gleason, coming to the edge of the light from the oil lamps and looking up the stairs. Shoot him, said a voice in Shaeffer's head, just gun him down and we can make all this go away. Gleason was unarmed, looking up at Shaeffer with a half-smile. 'You going to be a problem?' he asked. 'Like Mills?'

The wheezing sound returned, and Shaeffer looked down as something began to drag itself up the steps towards him. As it came into the light he recognised part of it as Mills: one side of its malformed face had the young soldier's features, one of its arms had the two stripes of his Corporal rank. But the other side... It was as if there was a dividing line running all the way down the soldier's body, one half was normal the other shrunken and rotted. The aged part of his face was a mess of desiccated skin and when it howled, turning a milky eye towards Shaeffer, yellow teeth fell from between black lips and scattered on cold stone steps like loose change.

'My aim was off,' said Gleason.

A gunshot rang out, and Shaeffer ducked as the bricks to one side of him shattered, a bullet having just missed him.

'So was mine,' said Mulroney from the shadows, throwing his gun to Gleason. Shaeffer fired two rounds at Gleason, but they were loosed in panic and he missed. Gleason moved out of sight, and Shaeffer pulled himself back through the open doorway. He slammed the door shut but there was no key, no way of locking it from the outside. He ran as two more shots splintered the wood of the door at head height.

No head start, he thought, no such luck for you. He ran through the hall to the front door and opened it as he heard boots running across the floorboards upstairs.

Outside he circled the building, moving to the rear where the windows were boarded up. At least that way they wouldn't have a line of sight on him from the house.

Hopefully they wouldn't risk shooting at him out here in the open, he thought running as fast as he could towards the external wall.

As he reached it and vaulted himself up over it a shot skinned his shoulder. That answers that then, he thought, dropping to the ground and running as fast as he could.

Eight

Rex parked the hire car at the end of the track leading to the Hernandez House. If Gleason and his unit were at the address in the Cuban's pocket then he didn't really want to drive up to their front door in his little Renault. Size of the thing, they'd probably pick it up and throw it at him.

He wasn't altogether convinced they would be, though. If they wanted him dead, they were a crew of trained soldiers, why hadn't one of them come and attempted the job? Why hire local muscle? It seemed pointless. Still, whoever had hired the man, Rex was happy to meet them, if only to offer them a friendly punch in the face.

On the other hand, he could be strolling into somewhere that had no bearing whatsoever, a random address the Cuban had had cause to visit. No matter, it was the only lead he had to follow, so follow it he would.

The track was open with no real cover. Rex moved off into the undergrowth, circling around the old house so he could approach it from the rear.

He moved at a crouch, gun in hand. It wouldn't look good if he turned out to be sneaking around the garden of a perfectly blameless resident, but he'd rather be embarrassed than dead.

He reached the rear porch. Despite its poor condition, he could tell it was lived in. The trash bin was fresh, flies circling the remains of food packaging. A half-empty glass of iced tea sat on a foldout table, a tatty deckchair placed next to it. Someone just stepped inside, maybe?

Rex broke cover, keeping close to the building as he slowly climbed the couple of steps. As he put his weight down on the old wooden boards they creaked and, before he could stop himself, one foot went right through. Rex just about stifled a yell as the wood cut along his ankle and shin. He squatted down, keeping his eye on the house as he placed his gun on the floor, put both hands flat on the boards and levered his foot free. He just managed to keep his shoe.

'Nice and smooth' he muttered. 'Lucky not to have my ass shot off.'

Treading more cautiously now, he moved to the back door. A rickety frame covered in a mosquito net restricted his view through the open door. He kept his shoulder to the wall of the house as he gently pulled it open and stuck his head and gun through the gap. Lying on the faded linoleum of the kitchen floor was an old woman, mouth wide open so the gathering flies could dip.

Rex stepped inside, moved over and checked her pulse. Nothing. He lifted a heavy arm, still supple, and still quite warm. She hadn't been dead long.

He moved out of the kitchen and into the small front room. A large, cross-stitch picture of Jesus, yellow-cotton sunbeams framing his holy head, stood on the far wall, surveying the state of the rest of the room. Surely it would test even this man's alleged forgiveness, the place was a dump. A brimming ashtray held cigar butts, like stubby brown dog turds, a pair of easy chairs supported little but dust. A rug, draped across the wooden floor, had several holes in it where the threads had worn through.

Rex moved to the far end of the room where a staircase climbed up to the next floor.

Keeping his gun on the move, he ascended the steps, treading carefully in case of unreliable boards and came out onto a small landing with two rooms leading off it. The first was the old lady's bedroom, everything was nicotine-stained lace and faded floral wallpaper.

Next door was a kid's room, a handful of toys on the floor, a few posters on the wall. Lying on the small bed was a young boy. Rex, knowing what he was going to find, reached for a pulse and found none. The boy's face was pained, teeth and lips pulled back in a rictus. Whatever had killed him had done so quickly but painfully. There was no sign of any external wound, so Rex had to assume poison. He looked around and saw a half-full glass of iced tea, just as there had been downstairs. Rex picked it up and sniffed it. There was a chemical odour there, beneath the sugar and lemon. He put the glass back down and went downstairs. Had the Cuban killed them before coming to see him? If so, why? Rex found it hard to imagine that either the boy or the old woman could have presented a threat.

He heard a car coming up the track. Keeping back, peering past the old net curtains, he saw an old man stepping out of a taxi a few feet away. The taxi turned off its engine and stayed put as the old man made his way down the track to the old house. He was dressed smartly, a light grey suit and tie, a panama hat to keep the sun from his eyes. The old man walked up to the house, climbed the couple of front steps and walked over to a rickety-looking swing chair on the far end of the porch. He pulled a handkerchief from his breast pocket and whipped away a little of the dust from the chair's seat. It was half a job, it was dirtier than anything less than an axe could fix. Nonetheless, he pulled a contented face and sat down, the springs crying out as if he had kicked them.

'I know you're in there, Mr Matheson,' he said. 'Might I suggest you come out in the fresh air. The smell in there is quite beyond me, I'm afraid.'

Rex thought about it for a second then moved to the front door and let himself out.

'Much better,' said Mr Wynter. 'I'd offer you a seat next to me, but I'm not sure this thing would take both our weights.'

'That's fine,' said Rex. 'I'll stand.' He moved beyond the swing seat so that the driver of the cab wouldn't have a clear line of sight on him. Just in case.

They looked at one another for a while, summing each other up.

'You can call me Mr Wynter,' the old man said eventually. 'I work for the government.'

'Whose?'

'Yours.'

'Well, that's a relief.'

'Indeed, Mr Matheson. I am employed as something of a free agent. I clean up other people's mess.'

'Lot of that around here,' said Rex, nodding towards the house. 'That you?'

'I'm not one for witnesses.'

'That include me?'

'Of course. But not yet.'

'Maybe I should just shoot you now then, make life easier for me down the line.'

'Mr Matheson, I have cradled the leaking brains of presidents in my bare hands, do you really think you've got what it takes to intimidate me?'

'You're the one offering threats.'

'I was aiming for a disarming honesty.'

Rex twitched his gun. 'You failed. Whose mess are you clearing up?'

'Oh, the usual mistakes of government. Nothing that need concern you in detail. Certain equipment was purchased; said equipment is now in enemy hands.'

'Colonel Gleason.'

Mr Wynter inclined his head in agreement. 'I'm just here to make sure that everything we have paid for is accountable and that anyone who has seen it doesn't live to talk about it.'

'You on your own?'

'Yes.'

'Then good luck. I don't imagine you'll have any more luck scaring Gleason than you do me.'

'I'm not trying to scare you, Mr Matheson, it's not my way. You're not an idiot, and I choose not to treat you like one. I am here doing my job. Right now you are more of a help than a hindrance. When that changes, then you are a loose end and I will kill you.'

'Unless I kill you first.'

'Indeed. Always a possibility. In the meantime, we will each get on with our business and go about the saving of innocents in our own way.'

'What's to stop me just calling in my superiors and having you put away?'

'The more people you tell about me, the more people will eventually disappear. You're not a naive man.'

'Just an incredulous one. I don't believe every spooky old guy that tells me he's the ultimate assassin.'

'Then ring up your delightful watch analyst, Esther, and see how long she lives after you discuss matters with her.'

Mr Wynter got up and brushed off the seat of his suit pants. 'Anyway, I thought it only polite for us to meet.'

From the Hernandez House there came the sound of gunshots. Muted but recognisable.

'Ah,' said Mr Wynter. 'I think you're about to get busy.' He fished in his suit pocket for Penelope Lupé's cellphone. 'I've decided to give you this.'

Rex took it. 'Why?'

'I'm feeling helpful.'

There was another gunshot, in the open air this time. Rex moved across the porch, eyes trained towards the source of the noise. He jumped down to the track.

Mr Wynter walked back towards his cab. 'See you again, Mr Matheson,' he said. 'Once more, anyway.'

Nine

'I got him,' said Mulroney.

'You barely winged him,' Gleason retorted. 'More shirt than bone.'

Behind them, Ellroy and Leonard appeared, carbines in hand.

'Oh, look,' said Mulroney. 'It's the cavalry.' He ran into the garden, sprinting towards the far wall where Shaeffer had fallen.

'What's happening,' Leonard asked.

'Shaeffer flipped,' said Gleason. 'Killed Mills and then ran.'

'Killed Mills?' said Ellroy

'You heard,' Gleason replied.

Mulroney reached the wall, jumped up and straddled it, gun in hand. He turned back towards them and shook his head.

Gleason beckoned him back. 'We're packing up and getting out, now.' He turned to Ellroy. 'Get the truck prepped. You...' turning to Leonard, 'clear upstairs. Quick, the clock's ticking.'

*

Rex had got to the gates of the Hernandez House in time to see Mulroney returning through the front door, and Ellroy pushing past him and heading towards one of the outbuildings. After a few minutes, there was the sound of an engine and a truck reversed out in front of the old house.

'On the run again,' Rex muttered, keeping tight to the wall and watching through the gates. Question was, what should he do about it? The truck was now blocking the front of the old house and providing cover for the men that moved behind it. Rex could see that they were loading their belongings into the rear of the truck. A few army packs, then a wooden crate, followed by another. There was a pause for a couple of minutes, then two more crates appeared. These were loaded aboard, two of the men climbing in behind them. There was a clattering of metal as they pulled the corrugated back shutter of the truck closed.

'I'll get the gates,' said the eldest – Gleason himself, Rex presumed – holding out his hands for the keys, which the driver yanked out of the pocket of his jeans and threw to him. The driver climbed into the front of the truck and followed slowly behind Gleason. Rex moved along the wall, clearing the far corner so that he was out of sight when the gates swung open and Gleason stepped out. He didn't bother replacing the chain, just threw the keys into the grass and climbed into the truck's cab. As it pulled away, Rex hoped to hell that nobody was looking in the wing mirrors and ran up behind it.

The truck didn't draw to a halt and nobody

came out to shoot him, so he guessed he'd got away with it.

The truck moved slowly along the mud track and it was easy for Rex to keep up. He climbed up the rear shutter, wedging his foot in a loop of plastic hanging from the handle and forcing his fingers into the gaps between the metal slats. It was far from the safest way to travel but he could just about hold on as the truck pulled onto the proper road.

The vehicle began to gather speed, and Rex could feel himself slipping so he pushed himself up higher and gripped the edge of the roof. Pulling himself up, he slid onto the roof of the truck, gritting his teeth as it bounced along the uneven tarmac. Once there he lay as flat as he could, hoping he hadn't made enough noise for the people inside to be suspicious. If he could stay where he was, he should be safe until they arrived at their destination. Then... well, he'd make it up as he went along. As a plan, it hadn't killed him yet.

He spread his arms and legs out, gripping the edge of the roof with his fingertips and trying to ride out the bumps without falling off or slamming against the roof.

The truck pulled up at a set of traffic lights and he relaxed for a moment, letting the cramps in his muscles ease off.

Then the cellphone Mr Wynter had given him began to ring. Loudly.

He snatched for it, hand caught in the pocket of his jeans as he tried to tug it free. Inside the truck, he heard raised voices and, peering over the edge of the roof, he saw Gleason's head appear out of the passenger window before pulling back inside. The truck engine revved and it pulled out into the oncoming traffic surrounded by the blare of car horns. Rex grabbed the edge of the roof as tightly as he could, his body spinning as the momentum tried to pull him from the roof. The truck began to speed up, overtaking the other cars on the roads, which swerved to accommodate it as it reared up behind them. Rex could guess what was coming. The brakes slammed on and Rex dived for the rear of the truck, grabbing the edge of the roof to stop himself from flying off the front and into the road. The metal cut into his fingers as the force threatened to yank his arms out of their sockets. He rolled forward and jumped down onto the road, his legs buckling beneath him. He pushed himself up, aware of the traffic coming towards him. A dirty, black Chrysler was bearing down on him and he jumped as it drove straight into the rear of the truck, unable to stop in time. Rex rolled over the hood falling to the road on the other side, getting straight to his feet and running towards the sidewalk, car horns and the shouts of drivers erupting all around him.

The truck, ignoring the Chrysler, drove on.

Rex limped his way off the street. He couldn't follow the truck on foot and the longer he hung around, the greater chance he had of the police turning up and arresting him.

Once off the main road, he sank down onto the sidewalk, waving his bleeding palms in the air. He wanted to put his whole body on ice. He looked at the cellphone. 'Missed Call' it announced. 'Oscar'. The penny dropped that this was Penelope's phone, taken by Wynter when he had killed her. Good timing, Shaeffer, you asshole, he thought. Then decided to call back and tell him in person.

Mr Wynter overtook Gleason's truck in the taxi and looked at the man's profile. His face was deep red, jaw clenched. His hand gripped the bracket on the rear-view mirror as if it were Rex Matheson's neck. Mr Wynter chuckled. Gleason was not a man who liked his plans interfered with.

'Go straight to the harbour,' he told the taxi driver.

Shaeffer lay still in the undergrowth at the side of the road. The truck drove past, and he saw Gleason in the passenger seat. Shaeffer kept his head down until he could no longer hear the engine.

After he was sure it was clear, he got to his feet and climbed back onto the road. He dabbed at his shoulder with his fingers. Nothing but a shallow cut, the bullet hadn't even nicked the bone.

He pulled the phone out of his pocket, carefully sliding the battery into place and holding down the power button. After a few seconds, the phone booted up and the screen came on. Impatient, Shaeffer shook the phone as it slowly initialised the contacts list, found a phone signal, welcomed him to the local roaming network and finally received a text message telling him how extortionate the call rates would be. To hell with it, he thought, it's not my bill.

He called Penelope's number and held on, waiting for her to pick up. It went to the answer machine.

'It's me,' he said. 'Call me right back.' He hung up and carried on walking.

After a couple of minutes the phone rang. He looked at the screen, saw it was Penelope and answered it.

'These people want to kill me, Penelope,' he said, 'so answer your damn phone when it rings. Where were you?'

'Having the same people trying to kill me,' Rex replied. 'Thanks to you.'

Shaeffer stopped walking in surprise, looked at the phone to confirm he hadn't misread the caller ID. 'Who the hell is this?' he asked. 'Where's Penelope?'

'Dead. Sorry, you know her?'

'No, I just—'

'Then I'm not sorry. She died because you called her, asshole, so it's on you.'

'Hey, no...' Shaeffer couldn't believe this guy. 'I was just... I wanted to do the right thing, you know? Screw you! How is she dead?'

'Some people don't like that you and Gleason are off the map. Where are you?'

'I'm...' Shaeffer looked around. 'Truth is, I don't know. Not far from the house where we were holed up, heading into town.'

'You on the main road?'

'Yeah, you know it?'

'Just driven down it, pretty sure I can back track. Tell you what, can you hotwire a car?'

'CIA Special Operations, pal, I can start a car by winking at it.'

'I just got shivers, you're so cool. Head back the way you came, top of the track is my hire car. If somebody even cooler than you hasn't stolen it already. Can't miss it, looks like it came free with a pack of cereal.'

'Hey!' Shaeffer shouted. 'You're being pretty up yourself for a guy that wants my help.'

'I could say the same thing about you. Now come down the road and pick me up, I'll be the bleeding black guy on the roadside flipping you the bird.'

'Keep talking like this, I'll run you over.'

'In that? I'd stop it with my foot. Now get on down here before we lose Gleason for good.'

Shaeffer found the car and put the passenger window through with a brick. 'How's that for super cool?' he said, reaching inside to unlock the doors.

He moved around to the driver's side, brushed away the small amount of broken glass that had fallen his side, got in and reached under the steering wheel. He pulled back the panel beneath and yanked out a bundle of wires, peeling them apart so he could see what he was looking at. He stripped back the two red wires and fused them together, then grabbed the brown ignition wire. He stripped it back slightly and touched the exposed piece to the joined red wires. The engine roared. Shaeffer revved the car to stop it from stalling and tucked the wires away as safely as he could.

He reversed onto the road and drove back the

way he had come. Within a few minutes he was out of the rundown area and back amongst the more frantic traffic. He saw, exactly as described, a battered-looking black guy with his middle finger raised towards him. Reluctantly, and to a hail of Spanish curses as he cut across traffic, he pulled over.

'Thought you'd piss some folks off, huh?' said Rex, waving to the drivers as he opened the door.

'Not my fault Cubans drive like they're at a fairground. Now shut up and get in.'

'Well, see, I'd like to,' Rex replied, "cept someone decided to put broken glass all over my seat.'

'Fat ass like yours you won't even feel it.'

Rex didn't even honour that one with a reply, just scooted the biggest pieces off the seat and climbed in.

'You know how to get to the harbour?' he asked as Shaeffer pulled into the traffic.

'No idea.'

'You came from there.' Rex held his hands in the air, exasperated. 'When you were on a boat. That thing that sails through water so your feet don't get wet. Remember?'

'It was dark and I was riding in the back of the truck, OK?'

Rex shook his head. 'Just one break,' he said, 'that's all I ask for, one decent break...'

'There!' Shaeffer pointed at a signpost across the way and followed it. 'Initiative.'

'Yeah, well, I hope your initiative is still working when we get there, I'd like to see how it works out in a gunfight.'

'Gunfight? The whole reason I called in you guys was so that I could get out safely, now you want me to go running straight back at them?'

'Given what you've told us about the weapons they're carrying, I'm not inclined to let them sail out of here.'

'Well, what about back-up?'

'Back up? We're the CIA. In Cuba. You figure out the logistics. If you're that scared, maybe you should just sit in the car while daddy goes and takes care of some business.'

'I've seen a hell of a lot more combat than you, asshole. But you don't know Gleason and, like you say, that's some serious weaponry he's got his hands on.'

'All the more reason we stop him before we lose him for good.'

Shaeffer gave up arguing and kept driving. By the time they arrived at the harbour, late afternoon had turned into evening and the light had become dull, poured thick over the boats, shipping crates and people.

'Can you remember where you moored the boat at least?' Rex asked.

'The public moorings are on the far side,' Shaeffer replied, steering the car carefully between the rows of storage crates. 'We could take the road, but I assumed you'd prefer the stealthy approach?'

'Stealthy is good,' Rex agreed as Shaeffer manoeuvred the car around the unloading freights.

*

Mulroney reversed the truck as close to the mooring as possible. 'Speed or subtlety?' he asked Gleason.

'Screw subtlety,' Gleason replied. 'Let's just get out of here.'

'Roger that,' Mulroney replied, jumping down from the cab and banging on the side of the truck.

Ellroy and Leonard climbed down as Mulroney walked over to their boat. He hoped it had been refuelled as promised; Gleason had known they might need to leave in a hurry. He hopped over the side and jogged to the bridge, turning on the engine and checking the dials. 'Juiced up and ready to go,' he shouted across to the quayside, turning off the engine and returning to the deck where he lowered the lightweight gangway so Ellroy and Leonard could clamber aboard with the first crate.

Gleason had moved to one side, looking around for signs of trouble. With Shaeffer loose, they needed to regroup before their position was totally compromised.

The harbour was relatively quiet, just a few of the big freight companies shifting pallets to the shore.

He moved back to the rear of the truck and helped Mulroney with the second crate.

'Where next, Colonel?' Mulroney asked.

'Time to go home,' Gleason said. 'Take the fight to them. The faster we go at this, the better chance of success.'

'Never give an enemy time to react?'

'Precisely.'

Ellroy and Leonard brought the third crate aboard and Mulroney and Gleason returned for the fourth.

It was as they were stepping back down from the rear of the truck that they heard the sound of a car engine roaring towards them.

'There,' said Shaeffer, pointing towards where Gleason's unit were loading up their small boat.

'OK,' said Rex. 'Pull over and we'll sneak up on foot.'

'Sneak up, my ass,' said Shaeffer, dropping the car down a gear and slamming his foot on the accelerator.

'What the hell are you doing?' Rex shouted as the car sped towards the rear of the truck.

'Banking on the element of surprise,' Shaeffer replied. 'Feel free to start shooting at them.'

Rex yanked down his window, leaned out and tried to aim a couple of rounds at Gleason. They went wide, embedding themselves in the packing crate he was holding with Mulroney.

'Where did you learn to shoot?' Shaeffer shouted.

'Somewhere stationary!'

Shaeffer aimed the car between the truck and the boat, forcing Ellroy off the quayside and into the water while Gleason and Mulroney ran back inside the truck still carrying the crate. As the car passed, Leonard was the only one to get a shot in, a couple of rounds taking out the rear windshield and embedding themselves in the dashboard.

Shaeffer slammed the steering wheel hard to the right and yanked the handbrake. The car went into a spin past a row of crates, screeching to a halt behind the cove.

Rex staggered out into a fug of burned rubber and brake fluid. 'I'd shoot at them,' he said, raising his gun 'but I may need to throw up first.'

'Could have been worse,' said Shaeffer. 'I thought I was going to roll it.'

They took up position behind the crates, looking for a clear shot. Leonard had jumped aboard the boat and was using the bridge house for cover, while Ellroy had vanished from sight, likely swimming around the boat to come up behind. Gleason and Mulroney were still inside the truck. Short of emptying his magazine blind into the side of it, he couldn't see what to do about that.

'So much for the element of surprise,' he said.

'Hold them down long enough the police will show up,' Shaeffer replied. 'Reckon we can safely assume we've made enough noise for someone to think of calling them.'

In the back of the truck, Gleason had come to the same conclusion. 'We need to move now,' he said, 'before whoever that is keeps us here long enough for the locals to weigh in.'

'Easier said than done,' Mulroney replied. 'You want to make a jump for it?'

Gleason shook his head. 'I had something a bit more violent in mind.'

He unhooked a crowbar from a rail in the back of the truck and prised open the single crate they had left. Rummaging through the packaging, he pulled out a short metal pole surrounded by four thin pipes. The whole finished in a black sphere and a selection of wires to which someone had attached a switch.

'Item 2A,' he said. 'Projected energy weapon.'

'Payload?'

'Let's find out.'

Rex and Shaeffer were just considering a break from cover when the entire harbour seemed to self-destruct. A row of crates not twenty feet away burst into flames, and they had no choice but to run.

'Fall back!' he heard Shaeffer shouting. Yeah, thought Rex, *no kidding*.

They aimed for the car but the sound of compressed metal and tinkling glass soon robbed them of that plan. Rex caught a glimpse of the little vehicle floating skywards, a ball of flames and blackening paintwork

All around them, stacks of pallets split and burned. Steel shipping containers punctured with a resounding clang, sending hot shrapnel into the air. Rex was aware of other people, dock workers, running alongside them as they tried to make it to safety. What the hell ordnance has that guy got? he wondered. Is he firing grenades? Missiles? Nuclear frigging warheads?

Explosion after explosion rang out, and all thoughts vanished. Rex's ears were whining, his head vacant and dreamlike, as he surrendered to the rational need to run and keep running.

Sirens began to sound, but his hearing was so hammered he wouldn't have heard them even if the emergency vehicles were running him over. All was distant and hollow, as if his head was deep underwater.

Every now and then he caught a glimpse of Shaeffer beside him, both of them running until they ran out of ground or luck.

His skin burned, seared by the fire on all sides.

Oh God, he thought, jumping up onto the road and still going, I think this is actually it. I die in confusion, just another terror statistic, a name on the scrolling bar of an enthusiastic piece of news reportage. This is the sort of event you should only see long after the fact, diluted through cheap mobile-phone cameras or long-distance aerial shots. It's the sort of thing you discuss with your friends, disassociated from it by the extension of the TV screen. You should never actually be in it. You should never be able to feel the flames on your face. Nobody could feel that and actually live.

But he did. Both of them did. Minutes later, lying on the hot tarmac, exhausted and terrified looking at the raging inferno that was all that was left of the harbour. They looked to one another, both still deaf, both still unable to think anything but a white noise of panic. They nodded, a mutual affirmation that, against all odds they wouldn't die. At least, not today.

By which point, Gleason's boat was pulling out of the harbour

*

Mr Wynter watched the destruction from a safe distance. He followed Gleason's boat as it made its way out to sea, watching the two men stood aft through the lens of his compact field glasses.

'Round one to you,' he admitted, looking at Gleason's smiling face. 'And that's not something I often concede.'

He had put altogether too much weight on Mr Matheson resolving things back at the Hernandez House. It wasn't the young man's fault, he admitted, but nor was it a mistake Mr Wynter would make twice. The next time he cornered Gleason and his men, he would deal with them himself.

As Leonard steered the boat out to sea, cranking up the engine so that they began to bounce along the waves, both Gleason and Mulroney looked back towards what remained of the harbour. The whole place was aflame, pillars of smoke rising into the air.

'Public announcement number one,' said Gleason. 'A proof of our intent.'

Mulroney nodded. 'What next?'

Gleason smiled, holding out his burned hand in the cool breeze. 'Public announcement number two.'

Nine months earlier...

'What are those things with the big heads?' Terry asked, looking down at his feet, thoroughly sick of clambering through the rubble that was all that remained of the Hub. 'You know the shiny-skinned fellers, all teeth.'

'Weevils?' Barry replied.

'That's the buggers,' Terry agreed.

'Why?' asked Barry, walking over.

'I've just stepped in one,' explained Terry. 'Half of one anyway. Must have been crushed when the wall came in.'

'Nice,' said Barry. 'Stain your boots, that will.'

'Smells of Chinese curry,' Terry noted. 'One of those cheap ones that come in a tin.'

'Obviously as classy as you, then,' Barry said, scratching at his beard and prodding a pile of wet offal with his biro to make sure it was dead.

Terry pulled his boot free and tried his best to wipe off the remains in the Weevil's dusty hair. He walked gingerly towards the far wall, supported himself with one hand and checked the sole of his boot.

'It's all in my treads,' he complained, shuffling as he lost his balance and grabbing for a metal rod that was sticking out of the concrete wall. The rod swung back revealing a deep compartment.

Barry laughed as Terry fell over, and walked across to see what he'd accidentally uncovered. He reached inside and pulled out what looked like a rifle that had been fished out of the sea, all seaweed and barnacles.

'What is it?' Terry asked, getting to his feet.

'No idea,' Barry admitted before dropping the rifle in surprise. 'It gave me a shock,' he explained, 'like it was live or something.'

Terry prodded it with the toe of his dirty boot. 'Get your gloves on,' he said. 'Commander Jackson said no risks, yeah?'

'Risks?' said Barry, pulling on heavy-duty gloves. 'They're not paying us enough to take risks.' He hoisted the rifle into a thick plastic sack. 'Look at the state of it – Captain Birdseye's blunderbuss. Can't imagine anyone would have much use for it.'

Ten

Jimmy Lane was trying to force down one more tongue-full of ice cream. It was a sun-melted mix of Belgian chocolate and maple syrup, and the odds of him being able to stomach even a single lick more were not good. But what kid of 8 isn't brave enough to try when ice cream of this quality is at stake?

'When's this thing get started?' he heard his dad ask, shifting awkwardly from one foot to the other as he waited for the parade to begin.

'Any time now,' his mum answered. 'They don't run late here, it's part of the magic.'

'Part of the magic, my ass,' his dad replied. 'Probably get sued by whatever union people join when they spend their days dressed as cartoon characters. "Unfair exposure to mouse-head heat exhaustion" or "developed mange due to elongated beaver imprisonment".'

'Shush, honey,' his mum said, giving his dad a clip on the arm. 'Jimmy's listening.'

'No, I'm not,' Jimmy replied, dipping his tongue

in what remained of his ice-cream cup but not quite daring to swallow.

'No, he isn't,' said his dad. 'Besides, he's not stupid, he knows they're not real.'

'They are so!' said his mum.

'Christ, Mary, you're worse than he is.' There was a long pause. 'When does this thing get started, anyway?'

'I told you,' his mum replied. 'Soon. They have to wait until it gets dark.'

'It *is* dark.'

'*Properly* dark. Otherwise the floats don't look so good.'

'That would never do.' His dad scratched at a heat rash on his belly. 'There's got to be better things to do in Florida at night than look at lit-up dragons and elephants. We should have gone to one of those mediaeval things like last year.'

'So you could stare at the serving wenches again? I don't think so. It was embarrassing. Watching you sat there with a half-boner, face greasy from fried chicken. It's not my idea of a good night out and that's for sure.'

'Jesus, Mary, Jimmy's listening!'

'No, I'm not,' said Jimmy and, true to his word this time, he phased out their lazy argument and waited for the parade to begin.

The air smelled of food stalls, fried onions and cotton candy.

He knew the glossy Americana of the shop fronts and city hall was as false as the characters that populated it. He also knew that the magic castle in the distance was a trick of forced perspective, a castle of the imagination, no more. He was sickly from sweet foods, and his eyes were tired, struggling to focus on the thousands of fairy lights that had sprung to life around them. For all of that, even with his parents still arguing behind him, he found himself ready to believe the night could bring anything.

He was quite right.

'Can you do it?' Gleason asked impatiently.

'I think so, Colonel,' Leonard replied, flicking between the sheets of paperwork they had removed from the weaponry files. 'This should definitely pick up the psychic projections and manifest them so everyone can see them. Definitely.' Leonard shook his head. 'Who am I kidding? Not definitely. But I *think* it will.'

'I need better than "think", Sergeant.'

'Sir, I'm trying to hook up two pieces of alien tech using spares from an electrical repair shop. My only guide is the research notes of a lunatic captain, who keeps breaking off from his findings to reminisce about old boyfriends. This isn't standard field engineering, sir.'

'Just get it right.'

Leonard bit his tongue and continued to work.

Mulroney walked over, camera in his hand. 'Ready to make movies, sir?'

Gleason nodded. Mulroney raised the camera and stuck up his thumb to show it was recording.

'Wise men of America,' said Gleason directly into the camera lens, 'who sit behind your desks and decide how best to run this world. Listen and listen well. Because I am here to teach you a lesson.'

The floats began to move, a pre-recorded fanfare drawing a roar from the gathered crowd.

'Would you look at that?' said Jimmy's dad. 'Finally, they start.'

Jimmy wasn't listening. He was laughing at the twirling people in costumes, the loud song piped through the hidden speakers – a song from one of his very favourite DVDs as if they had *known*, as if they had read his mind. The chase of the lights as the electric parade worked its way past him was like a controlled firework display. It was a complete sensory overload and, mind reeling, he adored every moment. The light sculptures of his favourite characters flexed, and reached out to the crowd. It was animatronics, he knew that really, you could tell by the jerky way they moved. But imagine, he thought to himself, just *imagine* if it were real. It was the most wonderful night of his life.

Then the ghosts came.

They appeared everywhere throughout the park, all brought back to re-enact their final moments.

Richie Clemens, died October 1979, thrown from the roller-coaster he was riding in celebration of his 12th birthday. Children the same age screamed as he suddenly appeared before them, crashing into the fibreglass mountainside alongside their carriage in a cracking of young limbs.

Angel Collins, died March 1983 of massive

cardiac failure. Death has not slimmed her as she twirls amongst the parade dancers clutching at her failing heart.

Shadwell Barrett, thrown beneath the wheels of a parade float by his jealous brother in June of 1994. He bounces there again, his hands snatching at the ankles of the spectators.

Brad Lurwitz, depressed stuntman in the Wild West show, shoots himself in front of the crowd just as he did eleven years ago. It still gets the best response of his career.

Everyone who has ever died within the heavily guarded barriers of this pretend world is back on their feet and dying once more.

The living run. They scream. They chase towards the exits.

The small and the slow are trodden underfoot, many adding to the ranks of the people who died here. This includes young Jimmy, a confused half-smile on his face as if waiting for the moment that the trick reveals itself and the hidden magics become nothing more than concealed levers and tricks of the light.

That moment never comes.

A crackle, as the energies released in the air distort the camcorder footage.

'We're coming for you,' says Gleason, his face filling the frame, his eyes wild and filled with the reflected images of ghosts, 'and you will give us *whatever* we want.'

Eleven

'... and you will give us *whatever* we want.'

The video stopped and Rex closed the media viewer on his phone.

'That was in the mail inbox of every Section Chief in the Company,' said Esther. 'They wanted attention, they got it.'

'What's the party line?'

'Terrorist gas attack, caused mass hallucination and hysteria.'

'God bless the Age of the Terrorist,' said Rex, 'for, lo, it gives good cover stories.'

'And, of course, no link with Cuba. As far as CNN is concerned, that was just an anti-Castro demonstration. Fatalities in Florida were surprisingly low and the official line is: we wait until we hear some demands.'

'And the unofficial line?'

'Don't ask me. If there is one – and I'm sure there is – it's for higher ears than mine.'

'Which leaves us...'

'Absolutely nowhere. Broderick wants you to

file a report and walk away. Shaeffer's to report to Special Operations for debriefing.'

Rex sighed. He had known this was coming but it didn't make him like it any better. 'Hate walking away, Esther.'

'I know.'

He hung up and walked over to the bar table he was sharing with Shaeffer.

Eager to get out of Cuba, they had flown back to Nassau on the next available flight and from there to Miami. Now, booked into a small hotel in Virginia Key, they had planned to take twenty-four hours to decide their next step. It seemed their superiors had made that decision on their behalf.

'I'm not just strolling back in,' said Shaeffer, after Rex had passed on the details of the call. 'Debriefing my ass, I'll be wearing an orange jumpsuit and officially dead within five minutes of entering Virginia.'

'Get over yourself,' said Rex. 'This is the real world not *The X-Files*.'

'This from the guy who says he met Old Man Spook himself.'

'Just some old guy giving himself a rep he hasn't earned. We don't kill our own.'

'Grow up. That's exactly what we do if the mess is big enough to justify it. And this is one hell of a mess.'

Rex shrugged. He wasn't going to have this argument; neither of them would win. 'You think I like leaving it like this?' he said. 'It's unfinished business. The bastard tried to have me killed, hell, nearly managed it. If I could think of a way of hanging on in there a little longer I would. But the trail's cold, we wouldn't have the first idea where to start looking.'

'I do.'

'Do what?'

'Have an idea. Look, I worked with these guys for a good few years. I know how Gleason's mind works, and he sure as hell isn't going to just sit on his hands for a few days and then issue his demands. There'll be more fatalities. We know that nobody's going to just roll over and pay him because he freaked out a few holidaymakers. He knows the standing order: we don't give in to terrorism. So he'll keep pushing until he thinks we have no choice. Gleason gets off on it. You saw him in Havana, he'd do this even if he wasn't after money.'

'So?'

'So he kept saying that he'd take the fight to "them",' insisted Shaeffer. 'If you wanted to attack the heart of America where would you aim for?'

'The capital, you'd go to Washington.'

'Exactly. But Gleason's still experimenting with this stuff, he didn't get to finish in Cuba.' Shaeffer paused for a moment, remembering the sight of what had become of Mills, that half-wasted creature reaching for him as it dragged itself up the stairs. 'He needs to know he can control it,' he continued. 'He needs to perfect it.'

'So he needs somewhere to hole up,' Rex murmured. 'OK, where?'

'Mulroney has a place in Colorado. I don't know

precisely where, he played it close to his chest. Never really talked about it. I got the impression it was a bolthole, you know? Somewhere to run if life got too dangerous or he finally went too far.'

'You talk like he was always planning on doing this?'

'I think he probably was. Gleason and Mulroney have always been tight, there's the rest of the unit and them. And they've never been what you would call perfect soldiers. They liked it too much. Liked what the power gave them.'

'Liked the enemy's fear.'

Shaeffer nodded. 'It's part of it, we all know that, play up to it too. You want to scare the enemy. That's how you control them, how you beat them. You hear stories, like all that stuff in Vietnam, where troops would take over villages, set themselves up as king for a day. A lot of that is bull, the sort of stuff people spread when they want to give the army a bad name. It's easy to hate the man with a rifle in his hands, easy to think the worst of him. But sometimes it happened. Of course it did. People got a taste of power and it went to their heads.'

'And Gleason and Mulroney were like that?'

'Definitely. And they had an eye on profit too. Looting happens all the time, stuff just lies there, spoils of war, but Gleason and Mulroney weren't just opportunists. Sometimes they would plan around it. You know how much smuggling there is in Afghanistan, the Russian families get rich there through heroin. We were sometimes sent in to bust up a deal or wipe out a plant. There was a lot of money floating around places like that and I think Gleason and Mulroney took their fair share of it.'

'And you?'

Shaeffer shook his head. 'I wasn't perfect. I took plenty of booze and smokes over the years, but I wouldn't touch drug money. Besides, if there was a chance of that sort of thing, we'd always be kept at a safe distance. Like I say, Gleason and Mulroney were tight.'

'So you're saying he had this place as somewhere to run to in his retirement?'

'Yeah, which means there won't be an official record of it. The man's not stupid, you don't run off to somewhere the government knows about. It must be off the beaten track, somewhere he could spend the rest of his days without getting caught.'

'And it's in Colorado... You don't have any more idea than that?'

'Gleason once joked about him running off to God's garden. Whether that was a clue or not I don't know.'

'God's garden?'

Shaeffer nodded.

'Garden of the Gods is a national park in Colorado,' said Rex. 'You didn't know that?'

Shaeffer shrugged. 'Why the hell should I? Ask me about geography in the Middle East, I might have a chance, but I can't say I've watched much Discovery Channel the last few years.'

Rex fell silent, fiddling with his phone. He brought up a web window and searched for the

Garden of the Gods national park. He couldn't quite believe he was considering this. Though maybe he could get away with a short stopover on the way back to Washington?

'You know, we can do this,' said Shaeffer eventually. 'A couple of days below the radar, you seriously think you can't cover that?'

'What's made you so eager to help all of a sudden?' Rex asked. 'Back in Cuba, you couldn't wait to get as far away from Gleason as possible.'

'Then I found out what my government has in mind for me. Right now I have a better chance on the road with you.'

'If that's true,' said Rex, 'then you really are screwed.'

'So, we going to do this?'

Rex smiled. 'Why the hell not?'

Twelve

Mr Wynter sat in the private dining room of the Corazon Restaurant and patiently sipped at a glass of water. He looked out of the window at Ford's Theatre directly opposite. They were advertising a musical called *By George!* that promised to bring the illustrious history of George Washington to the stage as a 'madcap, musical romp'. Mr Wynter wondered if he had time to pop over and assassinate the artistic director before his employer arrived. Sadly not, he thought, as the door opened and a nondescript man walked in. His suit was off the rail, his overcoat thinning at the elbows, his briefcase worn at the corners. This was a man who didn't seem remotely important. Which was as it should be when you're one of the most powerful men in the country.

He shook Mr Wynter's hand and offered him a broad smile. 'Been a while,' he said.

'Indeed,' Mr Wynter agreed. 'I was beginning to think you'd managed to find a way to get along without me.'

'Never a chance of that I'm afraid,' the man replied. 'You can't run a country without breaking some heads.'

Mr Wynter laughed politely.

'I ordered the set menu,' the man said. 'I hope that's all right?'

'Fine, I'm sure.'

'It's very good. The chef knows his business.'

'And here was I thinking you chose the place because you were trying to make a point.' Mr Wynter nodded towards the theatre.

'Oh.' The man smiled, as if the location had only just occurred to him. 'I see what you mean. I dare say if Lincoln had been watching a "madcap musical", he may have welcomed the bullet.'

'In my experience nobody ever does.'

'No? Well I dare say you would know. I can't say I've been in that position.'

'No, you prefer to pull the trigger several states away.'

'Naturally. It improves my aim no end.'

'*Sic Semper Tyrannis*,' said Mr Wynter.

'Hmm?'

'Thus always to tyrants,' Mr Wynter translated. 'It's what Booth was reported to say just after he'd shot Lincoln.'

The other man smiled. 'We tyrants have always had a bad press.'

The waiter entered carrying two plates of shrimp salad. For a few minutes both men ate, Mr Wynter delicately forking mouthfuls of crab meat and shrimp.

'You know,' said Mr Wynter's employer, placing

his cutlery across his half-finished plate, 'I was reading an article about shrimp. It's put me off. Apparently they congregate around sewage pipes. It's where they breed.'

Me and the shrimp both, thought Mr Wynter.

The main course was hanger steak. The meat bled on their white plates.

'So what do you think will happen now?' asked Mr Wynter's employer, finally referring to the business in hand.

Mr Wynter chewed at his steak slowly. He found he suffered bad indigestion otherwise. 'I think Colonel Gleason is going to kill a lot more people before he is stopped.'

His employer nodded. 'We're inclined to agree. Such a pity you weren't able to deal with him in Cuba.'

Mr Wynter had been waiting for this. His failure was not something either of them were used to discussing.

'I spent last night looking at red-hot satellite photos of Havana in flames,' his employer continued. 'I was almost tempted to have them framed.'

'The weaponry in question was impressive.'

'So I hear. We've asked for more details from the Brits.'

'How are they taking the loss of their people?'

'I think they're more concerned we might stop our cheque.'

They finished their steak and waited on the dessert, a plate of beignets drizzled with Greek honey.

'I can't resist sweet things,' said Mr Wynter's employer. 'My wife tells me my cholesterol will kill me one day.'

'Something surely will,' Mr Wynter replied, brushing icing sugar from his fingers.

Thirteen

Gleason was dreaming of the dust. That first time in Iraq.

The desert had changed him, as it had so many people. The sand beneath your feet, the open sky that glowed so red at night you swore it was on fire.

The horrors were always there. The threat of gas attack, the promise of the Republican Guard, the rattle of the chain guns. But, for all that, Gleason had found peace. Marching invisible, relying on GPS because the sandstorms were so thick you couldn't see more than a few feet ahead. The distant crump of shells so soft and remote they could have been signals from another world. It was a soft world, a world for dreaming in as your hot hands wiped sweat on the metal of your weapon and the feeling of that solidity pressed against your belly was all that stopped you floating away for ever.

Gleason often thought of the death of Major Rider.

Rider had been his commanding officer on that slow walk towards Kuwait. A gentle soldier, one of the old breed fostered in peacetime. Rider talked about 'preventative measures' and 'respect for the enemy'; he bemoaned the failure of 'diplomatic solutions'. Gleason had considered him unfit for his rank. If you don't want dirty hands, don't go to war. He followed Rider under sufferance. He followed because of orders not respect.

'The man shits himself at shadows,' he had said one night, huddled with the boys under a tent roof, listening to carpet bombing in the distance. 'If we ever meet the Republican Guard, he'll be on his knees before they even draw a target.'

'The sand doesn't suit him,' said a young New Yorker Gleason had talked to a few times, Patrick Mulroney. 'It's just somewhere he used to lose golf balls.'

There was a ripple of laughter at that. But not from Gleason. He thought it was too true to be funny. He hated marching behind a man like that.

February of 1991, they were on the move just north of Basra.

The weather was cool for once, overcast with a threat of rain and as they marched out past the ruins it was as if a whole world had rolled over and died in the night. The remains of Iraqi vehicles formed a chain into the desert. Bombed-out tanks. Armoured vehicles spit open and smoking. From a distance, the dead convoy looked like the spine of a dinosaur revealed by the wind blowing back the sand.

Up close, the smell of death was more recent. The vehicles were not empty. Pieces of soldiers draped where the explosions left them. Half-cooked but blackened, like bad barbecue meat seared in the white-hot flash of the coalition's righteous fire. People left to smoulder and crackle.

As they made their way past the dead convoy, the sandstorm descended and they had to rely on GPS and the crackle of radios. They couldn't see more than a few feet to either side of them. The world had gone away and they were marching alone.

The first bark of gunfire had everyone in a panic. Nobody could tell where it had come from and they were frightened to fire back in case they hit their own.

Rider shouted for them to find cover, and Gleason went on the move, the sound of blood pounding in his head as he ran through the sand to the safety of an upturned jeep. It was like running underwater. He felt sealed off and numb. There was the sharp crack of rifle fire, tinny and lifeless, not the spectacular gunfire of movies but the real handclaps of hot metal flying through the air on the hunt for something to stop it.

'Keep to the rear,' he shouted into his radio. 'Stay behind the convoy, anything on the other side's a target.'

But the targets didn't come.

They returned fire anyway, hoping for a lucky shot.

The enemy raked the convoy with 30mm rounds and it sounded like a factory. The remorseless clang of riveting. The pounding bells of metal on metal.

If one of those hits you, it'll leave a hole, Gleason thought. One you'll be able to put your whole damn hand in.

'Return fire!' he shouted, wondering where the hell his commanding officer was. Wondering if Rider had run off and left them in this invisible war.

'Major Rider?' he asked his radio. 'Are you receiving me, sir?'

There was no reply but static, the crackle of open airwaves that reminded him of eggs frying in hot oil. That empty crackle could mean anything, it could mean that they were dead, they were gone, swallowed whole by the static and the dust and now it's just you. Here in the desert. Gun in your hands.

There was another burst of gunfire, and Gleason caught a glimpse of muzzle flare, no more than a few feet away. He took the shot, firing quickly before he had chance to lose the target. There was the flat sound of his rounds meeting a body out there in the dust, finding their home, burrowing out of sight.

There was more fire from his left. It was one of his own because his radio squawked and someone started crowing over their kill. Two down, but how many more?

There was silence for a while. Every moment fat with expectation. Every moment bearing the potential of renewed fire, of that one bullet that might kill you, the one that will turn the lights out and make the world as you know it just stop.

Gleason began to think it might be over. That it was just a couple of stray conscripts, lost and afraid out here in the storm.

He made his way out from behind the jeep and ran slowly along the convoy for a few hundred yards, listening out for anything but the strain and creak of his own pack, of the gentle thud of his boots in the sand.

He stopped behind the curled track of a tank and listened.

There was a noise. The soft crackle of the radio. That pop of eggs in the skillet.

He moved towards it, his side of the convoy, further out into the whiteout of the storm.

He knew he should stick by the vehicles, knew he would become disorientated out there where the wind was full of the desert and nothing could be seen. But that crackle drew him.

'Who is it?' came a voice. An American voice. Afraid, shouting out into the wilderness like a fool who has lost his way. It was a voice Gleason recognised.

'Major?' he asked. 'That you?'

'Sergeant?' Rider replied. 'Careful where you step, it's not safe.'

Gleason looked down but it was force of habit. If there were mines beneath him he'd only know when his size twelves landed on one. 'You stuck, sir?' he asked.

'Can't reach my radio,' the voice was close, just ahead and to the right. 'Got turned around in the storm. I daren't move. I think I'm stood on...'

Rider couldn't finish that thought; it scared him too much. Gleason didn't need him to. Gleason understood. Rider was spooked. He had either scared himself to a standstill or he really was on a mine. Either way, Gleason's feelings were the same.

'Why are you all the way out here, sir?' he asked the storm, moving towards where he guessed Rider would be. 'Were you running?'

'I told you,' the voice replied, and it was close, very close, Gleason would see him soon. 'I got turned around.'

'Thought you were running towards the enemy, did you, sir?' Gleason asked.

Rider didn't reply. There was a shape in the sandstorm ahead, and Gleason knew he'd found his commanding officer.

He walked right up to him, pressing up close so that he could see the look in Rider's eyes.

'It's all right, sir,' he said. 'I've found you now.'

He dropped low and checked the ground. Rider was right to be scared – his boot *was* stood on a mine.

Gleason stood back up. 'Bad news, sir,' he said. 'You've trodden in something.'

He laughed a little at that, though it was no joke, not to either of them.

'Can you help me, Sergeant?' Rider asked, and the look of desperation on the older man's face gave Gleason his first sense of what real power could feel like. He had this man's life in his hands and the appreciation of that was something that would change Gleason for ever.

'I can, sir,' he replied, drawing out his knife. 'I can help you.' He pressed the tip of the knife into Rider's thigh. 'How long do you think you'll be able to stand still?' he asked. 'Because you really can't afford to move. *Sir*. If you move, it'll go off, and it'll take everything below the belt, sir. You'll be a hollow man, sir. Spilling his brave guts in the sand, sir. Can you be still?'

'Sergeant...' Rider replied. 'Please...'

'Were you running, sir?' Gleason asked. 'That's all I want to know. Tell me the truth and I'll help you, but I need to know. Were you running?'

There was silence between them. The wind whistled. Somewhere, dropped on the ground, Rider's radio crackled. But there were no voices. Just for a few seconds, no words.

'Yes,' Rider answered. 'Forgive me.'

'No, sir,' Gleason replied. Slowly, not wanting to trigger the landmine, he lifted Rider's tunic and brought up his knife so the tip of its blade met the man's scared, sweating belly. 'Try and stay still, sir.'

He pushed the knife in halfway. It was a good knife, it slid in beautifully. He held it there for a moment, then withdrew it and ran.

He could step on a mine himself, he knew. But he was willing to play the odds, to enjoy a spin on the battlefield roulette as, behind him, his commanding officer, the weak and disgusting Major John Rider, tried to stay still while his life slowly bled away.

Gleason ran for twenty seconds before, behind him, there was the sound of the mine going off.

Gleason kept running, enjoying it. Loving the freedom of just pushing forward into the unknown, lost to direction and sense.

He stopped as he collided with someone else.

'Sir?' It was Mulroney. 'We thought we'd lost you.'

For a moment, Mulroney saw Gleason's real face, the wild look of a man who had found blood out there in the desert and thrived off the taste of it. It was a moment that would bond them together for the rest of their lives. Then Gleason dropped his mask back down, became the dutiful soldier once more.

'Tracking the Major,' he said. 'Tried to help, but he stepped on a mine. Nothing to be done.'

Mulroney nodded and Gleason thought the storm was stopping, he certainly found his vision clearing after what felt like years, maybe even his whole life.

'I'm sure you did whatever you could, sir,' said Mulroney.

They walked back to the rest of the men, navigating first with their radios and then, as the storm finally cleared, their eyes.

Part of Gleason is still walking.

Waking up on clean sheets, Gleason rolled out of bed and looked down on a body that was as scarred as his mind.

He walked into the en-suite bathroom and showered. He couldn't shake the sensation of being coated in sand, the dream clinging to him as it always did. He worked away at it with sponge, soap and nail until his skin was scalded and held the heat of the water even once he'd towelled off and dressed in T-shirt and jeans. He looked in the mirror and saw the pink face of an old soldier staring back at him.

'When will you just fade away?' he asked it. It didn't bother to reply.

Downstairs Mulroney was also up, wandering about the kitchen in his jockey shorts.

'Want some food?' he asked as Gleason sat down at the breakfast bar.

He noticed his commanding officer was not quite at ease with the day, a troubled look in his eyes.

'Something wrong?' he asked.

Gleason shook his head. 'Just not quite acclimatised, you know how it is.'

'Battlefield and bed roll then Colorado sunshine and French toast. I know. I've got juice too, unless that's a step too far.'

'Juice would be good.'

Mulroney poured Gleason a glass of orange juice and returned to whipping his eggs.

They'd been there three days now, and the heat of gunfire seemed a long way away. The ghost of a previous life.

Mulroney dipped bread into the eggs and laid the soggy result in the skillet. Hot oil hissed and popped, reminding Gleason of dead men's radios.

He didn't let the memory put him off his food.

Later, with Ellroy and Leonard woken up and

sent into town for supplies, Gleason and Mulroney stood beneath the big Colorado sky, dreaming up damage.

They took it in turns to use the rocks for targeting practice, first of all methodically working through the items they had yet to test and then just shooting off for fun.

'You think how different things would have been if we'd had weapons like this before?' Mulroney asked.

'Sure,' Gleason replied. 'With weaponry like this, we'd own the Middle East by now.' He let off a blast from a Sontaran handgun, ploughing a black furrow through the earth. 'We'd be swimming in oil. Still...' he said, dumping the gun on the grass and reaching for the Ytraxorian rifle, 'it's this that's really going to make the difference for us.'

'You love that thing,' said Mulroney. 'I'm not sure I see the potential myself. It seems too random. Don't get me wrong, it's powerful, I get that. But where's the fear? If we want to really shake up our previous employers, we want to threaten them with something that has the world shaking. Shooting people off into the sky seems a bit low-key.'

'Trust me,' Gleason replied, when I really let rip with it the world will shake more than you can imagine.'

Fourteen

Rex and Shaeffer landed at Colorado Springs Airport, having managed not to shoot each other on the flight, although it had been a close-run thing.

'When we get a car,' said Shaeffer, 'I'm driving. No way am I letting someone as highly strung as you behind the wheel.'

'Highly strung, my ass. Motivated is the word you're looking for.'

'Motivate yourself into an early grave unless you learn to chill out.'

The car-hire office was doing its best to cheer them up, all bright yellows and pastel blues.

'Hi there,' said the man behind the reception desk. 'My name is Albert. What can I do for you today?'

'We'd like to order a sandwich, Albert,' said Rex. 'This the right place?'

'Ignore my surly friend,' Shaeffer interrupted. 'He's scared of flying so it makes him all stroppy when we land. We'd like to hire a car, something compact but with a bit of enthusiasm under the hood.'

'I'm sure we can help you with that.'

'Thanks, Albert,' said Rex giving Shaeffer a homicidal look, before wandering over to a corner of the office to kick a plastic pot plant.

Once they had their car – and a brief argument in the car park as to who would be driving it – they headed out of the city and towards the open country.

The Rockies reached up around them, and they couldn't help but feel small as they wound their way through the landscape of dense trees and imposing rock.

'I feel like I'm in a Western,' said Rex. 'The sky's too damned big.'

They pulled in at the Garden of the Gods Park Tourist Centre and went into the gift shop to load up on maps.

'Think we could use some postcards, too?' said Shaeffer, browsing through a spinning rack. 'Maybe some novelty pens?'

'Had my eye on some of those coyote plush dolls myself,' said Rex, pocketing a couple of maps and his change.

They drove into the next town, Harker's Pond, and began cruising around for a place to stay. They eventually settled on a cottage motel on the edge of the town. What it might have lacked in amenities, it would make up for in privacy.

Rex rented the cabin furthest away from the reception office and they let themselves in, dumping their bags and sitting down on the beaten-up sofa in order to really enjoy their accommodation.

'This place has atmosphere,' said Shaeffer staring at a damp patch on the wall that looked to him a lot like Africa. 'I don't know when I last experienced such comfort.'

'It is beautiful,' Rex agreed. 'I just wept for joy in the bathroom, that son-of-a-bitch was so clean.'

'Thank you for showing me this glimpse into your hallowed life.'

'No problem, happy to share it with you.'

Rex unfolded one of the maps he'd bought and spread it out over the small dining table. 'Hell of a lot of ground to cover,' he said. 'This is looking more and more like a waste of time.'

'How can you say that when relaxing in such opulence as this?' Shaeffer retorted, looking to the corner of the room where a throw rug was piled up as if it had been trying to crawl away.

'And in such great company,' Rex countered.

'I was going to add that myself.'

'Given that Mulroney won't appear on any official records for the area, we're struggling to find a place to start. What we need is a map that actually shows all the ranches and farms in the area. That way, we can start to narrow down viable places. I can't imagine Mulroney's sunk his money into a Duplex in town, we're looking for somewhere remote. Somewhere he can avoid prying eyes.'

'Plenty of scope for that around here,' said Shaeffer. 'There must be a local office that would have registry papers, stuff like that.'

'Yeah... Time to spend some hours going over town records. How I love the rock and roll business of investigative life.'

Rex asked at reception for directions to the town hall before, reluctantly, heading into town with Shaeffer to do some research.

It took them the rest of the afternoon, skin grey from dust, to accept that they had bitten off more than they could chew.

'I'm so glad I agreed to this plan,' said Rex later as they sat in a local diner staring at a laminated menu without really reading it. 'I can't remember the last time I had so much fun.'

'Just wait until tomorrow,' said Shaeffer. 'We can do it all over.'

'I doubt I'll manage to sleep, I'll be so excited.'

'Doubt I'll manage to sleep either, though that will more likely be due to the fact that the bed's made of mould and gingham.'

They ordered almost randomly, pointing rather than reading, and hoping for the best.

A salad arrived. They poked it with forks.

'How did you get into this?' Rex asked. 'Toppling governments for a living.'

'Came up through the army,' said Shaeffer. 'Just kept saying yes when they offered me transfers. I've never been a man who planned a career path. You?'

'I planned it.' Rex stared at a coil of onion. 'Every single step.'

'Why CIA?'

Rex raised an eyebrow. 'Why not?'

Shaeffer shook his head. 'People don't just opt for intelligence work on a whim. I joined the military because it was easy for me, it was the path of least resistance.'

'And you're a least-resistance kind of guy.'

'Kind of ironic, given what I've done in my life. But, yeah.'

'If that was true, you'd still be with Gleason now.'

The waitress arrived with their entrées. If nothing else, it saved Shaeffer the embarrassment of replying.

The next morning, Rex woke with an idea. He took it outside with him on a hunt to find decent coffee.

'Esther?'

'Rex… Make it quick, a girl can lose her career talking to you right now. Where are you?'

'Colorado, saving the day as usual. I need you to access satellite imagery for the area around Colorado Springs, specifically the Garden of the Gods Natural Park and Harker's Pond.'

'Am I allowed to use the US satellite network as a personal Google Earth?'

'Sure you are. I need you to look for any unusual heat traces. They'll be centred on remote areas, ranches, farms, that sort of thing. Gleason's team are holed up around here somewhere and they will have been playing with their stolen toys for sure. From what I saw in Cuba, that stuff's going to light up a satellite image like Christmas.'

Esther thought about it for a moment. 'OK, but

I'm going to have to clear it.'

'Clear what you like, but don't set alarm bells off all across the network – the last thing we want is to scare him off again. We do that, we're never going to find him.'

Rex hung up and walked into a promising-looking coffee shop with an actual spring in his step.

'Well, look at you so happy,' said Shaeffer when Rex returned to the motel with a pair of coffees. 'You get laid while you were buying breakfast?'

'Nobody in this backward town could be so lucky.'

Rex told Shaeffer his plan.

'About time we started acting like we had the weight of the US Government behind us,' said Shaeffer. 'That mean we don't have to spend the day going through files any more?'

'What else you got in mind?'

'There's a UFO Watchtower a few miles up the road, thought I might settle in and see what flew by.'

'Yeah? Maybe see if they'll sell you some of their ray guns while they're at it,' Rex replied. 'Might even out our chances with Gleason.'

They ended up looking at old files anyway, just in case the satellite images didn't help. They had to do something to fill the time; Esther had made it clear how many hours they could expect to wait while she sifted through data.

At lunchtime, they left the town hall, just so

that they could breathe air for a while, and took a stroll down the main street of Harker's Pond.

It was a quaint little place, the sort of town that counted a night at the Lucky Steer – a particularly buttoned-down country and western bar they'd passed on their way into town – as the height of its social calendar. It was likely filled with ageing Republicans, Rex thought, as he browsed the racks of the general store, who all drove identical Oldsmobiles and ate at each other's barbecues on a Sunday. The sooner their business was done the better. If he stayed here too long the attitude might get to him. He'd start ironing a crease in his jeans, or nodding while Fox News was on.

'Just going to grab a pair of sunnies,' said Shaeffer, 'so I can try and look as cool as you.'

He walked over to a revolving rack by the front door, foraging amongst the clip-ons and mirrored aviators for something a little more his style. He grabbed a plain pair, put them on and then spun the stand around so that he could check his reflection in the small mirror fixed at head height on one of its sides. As the rack revolved, the mirror gave him a sweeping view of the street behind him. A barber's shop, a grocery store, a small café, its brightly painted sign proclaiming it to be the 'Cheery Bean' in letters of red and blue stripe. Just stepping out of the grocery store was David Ellroy, a couple of shopping bags in his arms. Right after him came Joe Leonard.

'Well now...' said Shaeffer. 'Why couldn't that have happened yesterday?'

As he was staring, Leonard looked across the

street and the man's eyes fixed on his back.

Stay cool, Shaeffer thought, don't let him know that you've seen him, too. Just check out your sunnies and relax...

Leonard grabbed Ellroy's arm and yanked him off up the street. Slowly, not wanting to be too obvious, Shaeffer moved the rack so that he could follow the two men down the street. They climbed into a navy-blue SUV and Shaeffer squinted, trying to read the license plate. No good. It was too far away.

He walked inside and looked for Rex.

'We've got to go,' he said, grabbing Rex's arm. 'Quickly. I've just seen two of our boys across the street. Problem is, they saw me, too.'

'Shit.'

'Yep.'

The two men ran out of the store and up the road towards the hire car.

'Give me the keys,' Rex shouted.

'It's OK, I can drive.'

'My turn to smash up a hire car,' Rex insisted. 'Hand them over before I shoot you.'

With a sigh, Shaeffer tossed them over and Rex pressed the button to unlock the doors.

They climbed in, Rex slipping the keys in the ignition and turning over the engine.

'No way we're going to catch up with them,' said Shaeffer. 'They've had maybe a minute and a half head start.'

'Minute and a half?' said Rex, slamming his foot on the accelerator and pulling out onto the road. 'I can catch that up in no time.'

The car roared up the street, a little old woman stepping out from the general store and chasing towards them.

'Who the hell is that?' Rex asked, swerving to avoid her.

'The owner, I think,' Shaeffer replied. 'Wonder what her problem was.'

Rex glanced at him. 'Look in the mirror, you dumb bastard.'

'Shaeffer flipped down the sun visor and realised he was still wearing the sunglasses, paper price ticket dangling to one side of his nose. 'Oops. Can you get me off a thieving charge?'

'Nope,' said Rex, shifting up the gears. 'I'll be in the next cell, serving a term for reckless driving.'

Rex aimed out of town and hoped for the best. Earlier, he had looked down his nose at the town and its parochial quietness; now he was glad of it. There was virtually no traffic on the roads and he could go as fast as the car was willing.

Shaeffer writhed next to him, pushed back in his seat, gripping the edge of it. 'Don't let anyone else pull out,' he muttered. 'I do not want to survive countless warzones only to end up creamed across the tarmac of the most boring town in America.'

'Chill,' said Rex. 'Put the radio on or something.'

'Radio, yeah, right, find something upbeat to scream along to.'

As they pulled out of the town limits, Shaeffer caught a glimpse of dark blue dead ahead. 'That's them,' he said. 'We might pull this off yet.'

Rex slowed the car down. 'Play our cards right and they might lead us right back to Mulroney's place.'

'Then what?'

'Then we save the world in a blaze of glory and gunfire.'

'Oh, OK. Just so as I know.'

Ahead of them, the blue vehicle also appeared to be slowing down and Rex was forced to put his foot to the brake again. 'What's their problem?' he asked as the SUV renewed its speed. Rex accelerated and the SUV charged ahead.

'They're onto us,' said Shaeffer. 'Checking us out, seeing if we'd match them.'

'Well what else can I do?' asked Rex. 'I can't afford to lose them.'

'Certainly not now, the minute they get back to Gleason and tell him we're here, the whole unit will be gone again.'

'And then we'll never track them.'

'You got it.'

'How do we know that they're not already calling him?'

'With what? No cellphones allowed, and I bet you they didn't take a radio just to go shopping. If we can stop them now, then we've bought some time.'

'OK,' said Rex. 'That's a plan. Hold on to your stomach.'

He kept the accelerator flat to the floor, the car shaking around them as he forced the speedometer higher and higher. The road was straight but not flat, the car leaving the road for several terrifying seconds as Rex crested a slight hill. Ahead of them, Ellroy and Leonard were also putting on speed, but their car was too big and heavy to be a match and Rex and Shaeffer slowly began to gain ground.

'They're going to realise that this isn't just about speed,' said Shaeffer, grinding his feet against the carpet of the passenger-seat footwell out of habit. 'As long as we don't run out of road, we're going to overtake them, so they'll need to think of something else to shake us off.'

'They can think long and hard,' Rex replied, feeling strangely calm as he kept the car moving forward at full throttle. 'This man's not for shaking.'

As the SUV grew ever closer, Shaeffer saw the sunroof begin to open and he realised what would come next.

'They're going to take a shot from the roof.'

'At that speed?'

'Wedged in the sunroof, wind to your back, there's worse conditions to get an aim.'

'I can't get any faster,' said Rex. 'This is flat out. We're gaining but not fast enough.'

Shaeffer began cranking open their own sunroof. 'Then I guess I'm going to have to try and slow him down. Somehow. With the wind full in my face. I wish you'd let me drive.'

He gripped the edge of the roof and slowly pulled his face above the edge, keeping one hand pressed against his stolen sunglasses, trying to hold them in place so at least he could open his eyes in the slipstream that was rushing over the car. He shuffled so that one foot was on his seat while his other knee rested on Rex's shoulder.

'Watch what you're doing!' Rex shouted. 'One thing a man does not need when driving at this speed is a knee in his face, it puts him off his steering. Hear me?'

'I'd gladly swap, asshole,' said Shaeffer, trying to wedge himself back against the rear edge of the sunroof, one hand laced over his sunglasses, holding them tight across his face, the other held back against his chest keeping the barrel of his gun facing straight forward. He figured that if he let the wind rush catch the gun side on, it would be out of his hands and clattering on the road behind them. It was not the most comfortable position to take a shot.

Ahead of them, Leonard was having a similar problem but in reverse, the wind forcing him face down towards the rear of the car. He was using one arm to try and brace himself upright, wedged against the rear edge of the sunroof, while his other, protected from the wind by his body, held his gun.

It all came down to who would get the first shot.

Shaeffer fired. The shot wasn't on target but it did crack off the roof of the SUV to Leonard's left. The recoil threatened to dislocate Shaeffer's wrist due to the awkward position in which he was holding the gun. Nonetheless, he didn't risk trying to move and just squeezed the trigger again and again figuring that quantity might be the way forward at this point.

The third bullet hit its target, taking Leonard in the chest. He dropped his own gun, and the arm he was using to brace himself crumpled, letting the wind push him forward.

Shaeffer shoved himself down into the car as he saw what was coming. Leonard's body, dragged by the slipstream, came forward through the sunroof and jettisoned from the SUV.

'Careful!' Shaeffer shouted, throwing himself to his right so as to give Rex room to steer. If they hit Leonard's body at this speed it would total the front of the car.

Rex dabbed at the brake, wanting to slow enough to grab a little extra control but not so much that he threw the car into a spin. He yanked the steering wheel to the right and then straight back again. The car skimmed the dirt at the side of the road but darted back onto tarmac quickly enough not to go flying into one of the fields that lay on either side of them.

Leonard's body, arms pulled back, face jutting forward, hit the ground with the briefest glimpse of red before becoming nothing more than a distorted lump on the white line in the rear-view mirror.

'One down,' said Rex. 'You want to pop back up there and shoot him for me too?'

Nah,' said Shaeffer. 'This one we'd better take alive.'

Ahead of them, Ellroy was weighing up his options.

He considered heading straight for Mulroney's

ranch, but there was no way he'd get there in time to actually warn Mulroney and Gleason – all he'd be doing was leading his pursuers right to their doorstep. And that would help nobody.

It was clear he couldn't outrun them. Both cars could keep driving along like this all day, but sooner or later they'd run out of road or petrol. He needed to shake things up a bit, change the odds somehow.

He reached for one of the shopping bags, dragging it upfront and dumping it on the passenger seat. There was a baguette poking out of the top which he tugged free and tossed onto the floor, rooting around blind for something heavier. His fingers grasped a tin of chopped tomatoes.

He lined the SUV up so that it was more or less directly in front of the car behind. They were creeping up closer and closer, and Ellroy could see Shaeffer's face in his rear-view mirror. Traitorous bastard, he thought. Lunch is on me.

He tossed the can up through the open sunroof.

'What the hell is—'

Rex had neither the time nor room to avoid whatever Ellroy had thrown. They were only twelve feet or so behind the SUV now, and if he tried to steer away he'd just lose control of the car. The object caught a glint from the sun, almost a cheeky wink, then punched through the windshield. Rex squinted against the spray of glass but forced himself to maintain control and speed.

'Can't see!' he shouted. 'Help a guy out here!'

Shaeffer was scrabbling for whatever the object was, fearing it was a grenade. If it had been a grenade, he realised, then neither of them would still have been driving along the peaceful highways of Colorado.

He turned back to face the front and, using the butt of his gun, knocked away as much of the broken glass as he could, opening up a clear space for Rex to see. 'Here,' he said, popping his sunglasses on him, 'you can even borrow these, if you like.'

'Real kind,' Rex replied, moving the car from side to side a little, hoping to present a more difficult target should Ellroy choose to throw something else.

'Tin of tomatoes,' Shaeffer said, holding up the tin. It was almost bent double, a thick strand of tomato juice leaking from where the metal had split.

'Whole or chopped?' Rex asked.

'Puréed now.'

'Unconventional.'

'And normally so good for you.' Shaeffer opened the window and dumped the tin out.

'Litterbug.'

'I was thinking of your rental insurance. Didn't want the juice staining the upholstery.'

'Nice.'

Another object came flying towards them, glass this time. The aim wasn't quite so lucky and it exploded off the hood, spraying thin gouts of liquid through the open windshield.

'There goes that upholstery,' said Rex.

'Yep.'

'Barbecue sauce,' Rex added, licking his lips. '*Cheap* barbecue sauce.'

'My ex-colleagues had no class. You see now why I had to leave their company?'

'You absolutely did the right thing. He starts throwing *Cheez Whiz* at us and I swear to God I'll shoot him dead, whatever you say.'

Rex finally brought his car right up behind Ellroy and nudged it with his front bumper. 'Pull over, you tasteless son of a bitch,' he shouted.

'That told him,' said Shaeffer.

'You want to talk him down, be my guest,' Rex said, slamming into Ellroy's car again. 'Right now, he's got me in a tetchy mood – I'm not feeling diplomatic.'

He bumped the car once more, then dropped back just short enough to start pulling out to overtake. Ellroy immediately swung the SUV to one side to block him.

'And this isn't helping,' said Rex.

The SUV slowed down a little, forcing Rex to do the same. Bit by bit both cars dropped back within the speed limit.

'What's he planning?' asked Rex.

'I don't know,' Shaeffer admitted, tensing the hold on his gun. 'Nothing good.'

The SUV burst forward again before swinging sideways on. Rex's car crashed into it, both he and Shaeffer flung violently forward against their safety belts. The air-cushions exploded, forcing them back against their seats.

As the two vehicles, now mashed together, slid along the road, Ellroy raised his gun to try and get a couple of shots in. But the momentum was too great and the SUV top-heavy. Ellroy tumbled backwards as the SUV tipped onto its side, metal sparking on the asphalt, as it slowly dragged the whole mess to a halt.

For a moment all three sat there, Rex and Shaeffer trying to breathe past the restrictive air-cushions, Ellroy twisted in his seat, shoulders pressed down against the door.

'What sort of dumb move was that?' Rex groaned, blindly grasping for the door handle so that he could climb out.

'Not so dumb if he'd managed to keep it upright,' said Shaeffer. 'If he'd done that, we'd have a bullet in our heads by now.'

'Maybe,' agreed Rex, then grinned. 'But he *didn't* manage to keep it upright, did he?'

They both climbed out, legs cramping, heads reeling.

Rex unholstered his gun and cautiously made his way towards the upturned SUV.

'You going to try shooting at me?' he shouted, 'or can we finally be reasonable about this?'

There was no reply, and Rex kept his gun firmly trained on where he now guessed Ellroy to be. Keeping the chassis between them for as long as possible, he came around the front, crouching low so he could peer around the vehicle and hopefully not get a bullet in his head if Ellroy was so inclined.

Ellroy wasn't. Rex could see him curled up,

piled in on himself with one foot poking out of the shattered windshield and the other thrust up against the passenger seat. Rex kept his gun trained on him all the same, shouting for Shaeffer to come over and give him a hand.

'You sure we should move him?' Shaeffer asked, looking at the bent-over body. 'He might have broken something.'

'He's broken my car,' Rex replied, 'that's what he's broken. I don't much care if the bastard's head falls off when we drag him out. In fact I'm thinking of dragging him out by the hair, backwards, through all that broken glass, just because it will hurt more.'

'OK,' said Shaeffer, holding up his hands, 'I guess as long as his tongue still works, we can get what we want from him. Maybe a little piece of brain.'

'From what I saw, he didn't have much of that to begin with.'

Rex kicked away as much of the broken windshield as he could and squatted down to reach inside. 'He so much as blows me a kiss, you have my permission to shoot him,' he said, reaching in to unclip the man's safety belt. Ellroy opened his eyes but didn't move. It was clear he considered Shaeffer perfectly capable of carrying out Rex's wishes.

'Can you move on your own?' Rex asked. 'Or do you need me to hold your hand?'

'I can do it.'

Ellroy pulled himself out of the SUV and onto the road, getting slowly to his feet.

'Nice driving,' said Rex. 'Especially loved the bit where you started throwing condiments.'

'Gleason close?' Shaeffer asked.

Ellroy just stared at him.

'Oh,' Shaeffer said. 'Going to be like that, is it? What a surprise.' He turned to Rex. 'You got a bright idea for getting us back to town?'

'As a matter of fact, I have.' Rex waved towards a small car that was coming up behind them.

The car pulled to a halt, and the elderly owner of the Harker's Pond General Store stepped out.

'Well now,' she shouted at them. 'Which one of you cocksuckers is going to pay me for those sunglasses?'

Fifteen

'You really think he's going to tell us anything?' asked Shaeffer. 'We're trained to withstand torture from the best, I don't think anything Harker's Pond Constabulary is capable of will make the difference.'

Rex was staring at the coffee that had just been dribbled into a thin plastic cup for him by the station vending machine. 'Don't be so sure,' he said. 'This is a cruel and unusual place.'

Sally McHugh, owner of the General Store had mellowed a little – though not much – once she had been convinced that Rex and Shaeffer were on the side of the angels (achieved by paying for the sunglasses as much as by showing ID). She drove them and their prisoner back to town, commenting that they'd left one of their friends 'smeared all over the highway like roadkill' and if they wanted her to pick him up too then he was riding in the trunk.

He sat down to stare at his drink for a while.

'How long do you think we've got before Gleason

and Mulroney give up on their food delivery?' he asked Shaeffer. 'Gleason really love his barbecue sauce or is he hightailing it out of here as we speak?'

Shaeffer shrugged. 'He's not going to hang around. Ellroy and Leonard are expendable, and he knows a remote hideout is just an easy target once you know someone's in it. We may have a couple of hours.'

'Couple of hours,' Rex sighed. 'Not long.'

'Nope. Nothing on the satellite imagery?'

'Not yet, Esther's still working on it. But she had to take some time out in order to clean up after our mess.'

'What would you do without her?' said Shaeffer.

'You're kidding? It's her fault I'm here in the first place, she can work until she drops, for all I care.'

Rex had been forced to call Esther, of course. It wasn't a call that had gone well. Out of his jurisdiction and with no official sanction whatsoever, involving himself in high-speed pursuits and open-air gun battles had panicked her. She had hung up on him only to have Broderick call him back a few minutes later. Broderick seemed to feel that Rex wouldn't be working for the CIA for much longer. Rex thought Broderick was a sanctimonious asshole who was quick to cover himself when things went wrong. He'd explained as much to Broderick and then put the phone down when it became too loud and annoying to hold anywhere near his ears.

Rex stood up and dumped his coffee, untouched, into the trash. 'I'm going to have a chat with our mutual friend, want to come?'

'Why not?'

The local police chief had been hoping for another quiet day. This wasn't usually a problem, Harker's Pond not being a rowdy neighbourhood. He'd planned on putting in his hours, do a little paperwork, maybe talk to the school principal about plans for their upcoming anti-drug fundraiser 'School's Not for Fools!' then head home for a bowl of his wife's chilli and a night watching *American Idol*. He didn't like the songs so much, but some of those girls wore skirts that let you see their lungs quiver and he liked that just fine.

Then he had the CIA acting like the Dukes of Goddamn Hazard on his doorstep and that relaxing evening of spice for the belly and eyes seemed remarkably far away.

'I can't just let you interrogate him on your own, son,' he explained to Rex. 'There are laws that govern police officers like myself. I need to make sure all conversations are recorded, documented and witnessed. We are living in the age of criminal rights, yes sir, we are. You may not like it, can't say I do myself, but it seems the vegetarians, poets and beatniks exercised their right to vote, so now we have to do as we're told.'

'Look,' said Rex glancing down at the man's desk plate to get his name, 'Sheriff Willocks...' He paused and glanced down again. 'Dubert Willocks... That's your name?'

'It sure is. There a problem with that?'

'Not at all,' Rex replied, with only the briefest of awkward pauses. 'Just not a surname I'd heard before.'

'Or a given name,' commented Shaeffer. 'Dubert, it's unusual.'

'It's pronounced "doo-bear",' the Sherriff told them. 'It's French.'

'You're French?' Shaeffer asked.

'Nope.'

There was another slight pause.

'So the thing is,' Rex continued, 'this case is extremely time-sensitive, and the lives of many people are at stake unless I talk to our man there as soon as possible.'

'Oh, you can talk to him,' said the Sheriff. 'I'm just saying you get company while you do.'

'Well, see,' explained Rex, resisting the urge to beat this obstructive idiot to death with his own stupid nameplate, 'it's also extremely classified, so I'm afraid I can't allow that.'

The Sheriff raised his hands. 'Well then, I suggest you get one of your superiors to either sign off a B17 that waives the responsibility of Harker's Pond Constabulary in this matter or have him legally transported to one of your own facilities. As it stands, there's nothing I can do about it.'

Rex sucked air slowly through his teeth. 'You are obstructing an ongoing investigation here, Willocks, and your unwillingness to be reasonable—'

'Not unwillingness, Mr Matheson,' the Sheriff

cut in. 'No, not that at all. If my hands were free to choose policy in this regard, I'd happily hold the nails while you nailed that boy's scrotum to the chair. I am not a man opposed to strong-arm tactics when the situation requires. However, I do not choose policy, and my hands are tied by the laws governing this land you are so determined to protect. So might I suggest you call your superiors, as I say, and get the wheels of bureaucracy turning?'

'And might I suggest, Sheriff Dubert Willocks, that you're a pompous prick?'

'Way to go on charming him there,' said Shaeffer once they were sat back outside. 'I could see he was close to bending, especially at the end there. He's in the palm of your hand, for sure, your little pocket policeman.'

Rex ignored him, pacing up and down, with his cellphone in his hand.

'Esther?' he said once the call connected. 'I need you to either tell me you've found something or be willing to make the entire Harker's Pond Police Department go away. I am getting nowhere here and the clock is ticking.'

'Tell me about it, the system's alive with this right now. I no longer have access to the satellite imagery, I no longer have access to anything. It looks to me like the whole Company is on this, except you and me.'

'Broderick talked.'

'Of course Mr Broderick talked, Rex. This is not just your little mission, this is a potentially global terror threat. Apparently, there's a whole field unit heading towards you, and they'll handle things once they arrive.'

'Jesus, Esther, I'm almost on top of him here!'

In the pause that followed, Rex could hear Esther gathering up all her courage.

'Mr Broderick says you've, um, compromised everything by alerting Gleason that we're onto him so that he runs for the hills and nobody has a clue how to find him.'

'Not my fault, Esther!'

'The intel doesn't read that way. All people can see is an agent who's… got too big for his boots and nearly jeopardised everything. You're going to be the scapegoat on this, Rex.'

'Shit!' Rex flung the cellphone across the room where it smashed against the far wall.

There was a moment of shocked silence as everyone at the front of the station looked at him.

'So,' said Shaeffer eventually, 'how is Esther?'

Rex stormed past the reception desk and straight out back to the holding cells.

Sheriff Willocks was on his feet and running after him. 'Mr Matheson,' he shouted. 'I told you that you were not allowed private access to the prisoner until sufficient legal procedures had been adhered to.'

'Fine,' said Rex, 'you can come too. If we don't get an answer from this man in a matter of minutes, it's not going to matter anyway.'

The Sheriff thought about it for a moment then nodded to one of his deputies to open the door to the holding area.

He and Rex marched inside, working their way down the narrow hallway of cells.

'Where is he?' Rex asked.

'Last cell on the right,' Willocks replied.

Rex walked to the end of the corridor, stared through the narrow bars and then gave them an almighty kick.

Willocks followed Rex's eyes and his jaw dropped. The cell was empty.

Sixteen

David Ellroy opened gummy eyelids and looked at the old man standing in the narrow beam of the desk lamp.

'Who are you?' he tried to ask, but his mouth was dry beyond his ability to speak and all that came out was a meaningless tumble of sounds.

'Side effect of the drugs,' said Mr Wynter, proffering a plastic cup of water. Ellroy made to take the cup and became aware that his hands were handcuffed to the arms of his chair. The old man tipped the cup towards Ellroy's mouth and let him drink a few sips. 'Not too much,' he said. 'I don't want you sick.'

'Sick?' What the hell was so wrong with him that water would make him sick? And drugs? What drugs…? Ellroy was finding it hard to focus. Just as he thought he had gotten himself together, fixed on a thought and ready to act on it, his vision blurred, his head swayed and his whole body had the slipping, vertigo sensation that you got tipping over the peak on a roller-coaster. Except he wasn't on a roller-coaster, was he? No. He was handcuffed to a chair and an old man was talking to him.

'Where's Gleason?' the old man asked, a gentle smile on his face.

'Gleason?' For a moment Ellroy had to think hard. Who was Gleason? Then he remembered, and fear gave him a brief few seconds of clarity. 'I'm not talking,' he said. 'Do what you like.'

'Oh, I will,' Mr Wynter replied. 'And you will talk. Because you're not dealing with amateurs in the desert now, soldier, little Arabs with their splinters and their cigarette lighters. No. You're dealing with a professional.'

Mr Wynter pulled up a chair and sat down in front of Ellroy, his hands in his lap, small knees touching Ellroy's. He was close enough that Ellroy, even through the haze of drugs, could smell the sharp, clean scent of peppermint on Mr Wynter's breath.

'You'll talk, Mr Ellroy,' Wynter continued, 'because I am a very dedicated gentleman and one with a reputation that is fast becoming tarnished in this current business. They will say it is because I am too old, Mr Ellroy. And perhaps they are right. After all, I *am* old. Very old. But I am still the only man in my particular line of business. I am a department of one. And I work for the best, Mr Ellroy, not just the changeable faces you see on your TV screen or smiling at you from the cover of *Newsweek*. I work for *power*. I work for the men who buy and sell this world we're on time and time again for their own pleasure. The people who carve it up piece by tender piece and lay it out to be fought over. They watch the ants scuttle on that land, Mr Ellroy, then they sell the ants guns and watch them pull the triggers in the name of their gods and flags. And when the ants are all dead, we simply train more. Because that, Mr Ellroy, is how you run a business. War is good.

'And when those men want something – those terrible, terrible men who own your life so completely there are pieces of your soul stuck to the sides of their toilet bowls – when they want something done, something smoothed away, they come to me. They do this because I am good and because I know the real secret of the world...' He leaned in to Ellroy as if planning to kiss his neck. 'Nothing matters,' he whispered.

Mr Wynter leaned back and smiled. Again, that sweet smell of peppermint.

He stood up and walked out of Ellroy's line of sight, stepping into the darkness behind him.

Then he returned, holding a small metal tray. His hands were encased in rubber gloves and he wore a thick butcher's apron to cover his light grey suit. He sat back on the chair, the tray on his lap. On the tray was a shining clean knife and fork either side of a metal specimen dish.

'You are blessed to know me, Mr Ellroy,' Wynter said in quiet, holy tones. 'I'm the man who held Oswald's hand when he was full of doubts. I'm the man that signed off on the Phoenix Program with a glad heart. I'm the man who agreed the price per kilo with the Contras, then bumped a rail up my nose while they machine-gunned their enemies. Machine-gunned them with the weapons our money bought.' Wynter leaned in close. 'I'm the secret policeman, Mr Ellroy. I'm what all the clever spooks have nightmares about.' He picked up his knife and fork and leaned in close. 'And I'm very hungry.'

Mr Wynter arrived at Mulroney's ranch half an hour after his prey had flown. The front door was open and the house empty.

He sat down on a wooden bench that looked out over the fields beyond, pulled his cellphone from his pocket and dialled.

'They're gone,' he said. 'But only just. I want every eye in the sky to be gazing down on the roads between here and Washington. They're coming to get us and we must be ready.'

Six weeks earlier...

Mr Black sighed impatiently and ran his finger down the itemised list of technology that had been prepared for sale to the Americans. All seemed perfectly fine; why he had to get governmental approval, he didn't know. After all, in matters like this it was the Department's responsibility. The Department sustained, governments came and went. Especially this one.

'He'll see you now,' the PA announced, offering Mr Black a smile she clearly practised in the mirror.

'Oh, will he?' replied Mr Black. 'How gracious of him. Please tell me you've at least freed up five minutes with the boss? I don't want to have to go through this twice.'

The PA's smile flickered slightly but she swiftly fixed it back in place. 'He has the full authority of the PM, Mr Black, as you are aware.'

Mr Black sighed. Two meetings with the King of Also-Ran in one week, he must have annoyed the universe for it to be treating him this badly. Reluctantly, he nodded at the PA and followed her along the corridor to the office. He ushered her out of the way and strolled inside, dumping the paperwork on the desk and going to look out of the window while he waited for the necessary signatures.

'Mr Black,' said the man behind the desk. 'Must I ask again that you treat me with the respect I deserve?'

'I wouldn't,' Mr Black replied. 'If I was treating you with the respect you deserve, you'd never get the stains out of your suit. Now sign off my paperwork so you can get back to being deputy arsehole and the rest of us can do some proper work.'

The other man gave a roar of anger and slammed his fist on the blotter. 'I will not be spoken to like this!' he shouted. 'I occupy one of the highest offices in this country, and I demand that people acknowledge the fact.'

Mr Black charged across the office, grabbed the man by his boring tie and yanked his head sharply down so his forehead banged off the surface of his desk.

'You can't—'

Mr Black proved him wrong by bouncing his face off the desk blotter again. This time it gave him a nosebleed.

'Want me to do it again?' Mr Black asked, 'because I will if you want me too, or you can just juice up those cherry lips of yours and kiss my arse if you prefer?'

'I am—'

'Nothing,' interrupted Mr Black. 'You are a caretaker, a man who holds the coats while the rest of us get on with the important stuff. Let me tell you a secret about power: if the dickheads on the street can vote you out, then you don't have any.'

Mr Black straightened the politician's yellow tie for him, plucked a couple of tissues from a box on the desk and handed them over so he could wipe his face.

'Now,' he said, his voice light and charming. 'Here is the list of the technology we're proposing to sell to the Yanks. I'll remind you that your… government wants this sale; we're raising you rather a lot of cash. Would you kindly glance at the list, then sign your name at the bottom so I can finalise arrangements?'

The politician looked at the sheet.

'What's an Ytraxorian Reality Rifle?' he asked, scrolling through the list.

'Nothing you need worry about,' Mr Black replied. 'If it was worth keeping, we wouldn't be flogging it. If memory serves, it's an unreliable lump of junk. Not that those don't have their uses.' He smiled and handed the politician his pen. 'As you're about to prove.'

Seventeen

'Where's Mikey?' Larry Gulliver asked, running around the kitchen, tie half-slung, briefcase and jacket under his arm. He rammed a piece of toast in his mouth and then regretted it as he tried to shout around it and nearly choked.

'One day,' his wife said, appearing calmly in the doorway, 'you'll set your alarm five minutes earlier and save the DEFCON 4 emergency every morning.'

'Where would be the fun in that?' Larry asked, retrieving the toast from his mouth and giving her a smile smeared with butter and honey.

She gave him a look of mock-disapproval and nodded towards the front door. 'Your son awaits you, as patiently forgiving as ever, in the safety seat. Now go!'

'I'm going! I'm going!'

She tutted as his kiss left honey on her cheek and he dashed off, juggling his case, jacket and toast as he fought his way past the front door and out onto the driveway.

'Hey, Mikey,' he said, opening the back door and dumping his case and jacket next to the little red safety seat. 'Try and be a bit more prompt, would you? You nearly made me late.' He gave his son a big grin. His son thought about it for a moment and then grinned back, shooting out both of his little hands and cooing. 'Jazz hands!' his dad said, which made little Mikey do the same move again.

Larry got in the driver's seat, started the car and pulled out onto the quiet, suburban street.

'Mikey,' he said, slowly working his way towards the Interstate, 'don't forget we've got the Leatherman presentation today, OK? So I need you to be on top form. You feel confident?'

Mikey gave a whoop from the back seat.

'Or I guess I could do it and you just chill with Grace in childcare?'

Mikey whooped again.

'If you're sure. I don't want you calling Jimmy from accounts a dick-limpet again though, OK? I think it hurt his feelings.'

Mikey whooped.

Larry put the radio on. 'Let's find some tunes,' he suggested and grinned as Mikey offered jazz hands again from the back seat. 'That's right my man, something with a bit of class.' He pressed the program button for KUVO, his favourite of the handful of local Jazz stations and began to play along to Duke Ellington on the patented Larry Gulliver Mouth Trumpet. On the back seat, Mikey chuckled along.

Traffic began to get heavy around them as they got closer to the city. Larry pulled onto Interstate

25 and tried not to let it bother him.

Duke Ellington switched to Miles Davis, Miles Davis switched to Stan Getz. Larry took it all, singing, trumpeting or drumming on the steering wheel.

In the back, Mikey whooped. Fell asleep. Then woke up and whooped again before dribbling slightly and falling back asleep.

Business as usual on the Larry Gulliver morning run.

Over Denver a decent morning was shuffling into a more surly mood. It just couldn't decide whether it wanted to shine or rain.

The cars flooded in regardless. They would soon be stuck in their offices anyway – to hell with what the sky wanted to do with itself.

Ahead lay the Mousetrap, the major highway intersection north of the city. It had got its name when a traffic reporter, looking down from his news helicopter, noted that traffic would often come in but not easily get out, the sharp turns notorious for tipping lorries that took them too fast. The city rebuilt it in the end, after a Navy vehicle spilled there, toppling six torpedoes onto the highway. When one of those torpedoes started leaking, the locals really began to panic. It turned out be nothing, but the fear lingered and the city planners stepped in, softening those curves, widening those lanes. Now, fewer lorries tip over, but the traffic was still one snarled-up son of a bitch.

In fact, many of the locals would happily bend your ear about the complex routes they take in order to avoid the place. 'The Mousetrap?' they say, laughing. 'Wouldn't be caught dead in it.'

At 8.17 that would become a very apt turn of phrase.

An hour earlier, the news helicopter for Channel 7, Denver's ABC affiliate, was prepping to take off for the traffic report. The morning's 'roving eye on the roads' would be, as always, the velvet-voiced Tom Washburn, a contrary bastard when the hangover was really pounding but a favourite with the ladies because, say what you like about radio, Tom had the looks for it.

'Come on!' shouted Jamie Kelver, the chopper's pilot and not a patient man in the mornings.

'Hold your goddamn horses,' muttered Washburn working on that bedroom growl the lady drivers loved with a shot of espresso and the tail end of a Philip Morris. 'You're not the talent, you're just the man that gets it from A to B.' He looked out over the city and felt a sense of ownership. 'Today nobody moves without my say-so,' he told the view, before flicking his cigarette butt off the roof and strolling towards the open door of the chopper, the rotors of which had impatiently begun to spin.

'Shouldn't throw things off a roof this high,' said a voice in his ear before the helicopter engine got so loud he could hear nothing at all. 'It might hurt someone when it hits the ground. Tell you what...' Washburn spun around, coming face to face with the sunburned face of Corporal Cotter Gleason, late of the United States Army, 'why don't you pick it up?'

Washburn didn't enjoy his last panoramic view of the city, it was over too quickly and he had his mind on other things.

Kelver didn't see any of this. He was too busy rueing the day he'd started working with Tom Washburn and running through his pre-flight checks. The first he knew about things being different this morning was when his door opened and a man dragged him out and to the ground.

'What the hell?' he shouted, thinking Washburn had finally flipped and gone Peter Finch on him.

It wasn't Washburn, it was Lieutenant Corporal Patrick Mulroney, and he wasn't 'mad as hell' either – quite the reverse. He laughed himself silly as he yanked the pilot's headset off Kelver's head and put a bullet in the pilot's left eye.

'You hear me?' he said into the mouthpiece, the roar of the helicopter engine now more than conversation could bear.

'I hear you,' Gleason replied, pulling his own headset into place and climbing into the back of the helicopter, the Ytraxorian rifle clasped firmly in his hands. 'Let's go.'

'Roger that.' Mulroney climbed into the pilot's seat and took over where Kelver had left off. 'When this is over,' he said, 'remind me to buy myself one of these will you? I just love 'em!'

The helicopter lifted gracefully from the roof and headed out over Denver's early morning skyline.

Once upon a time, Leonard Weisman would have

loved a downtown address in Denver. A bit of history, a little class, certainly better than the dump he'd spent ten years in when married to Velma. Actually, he thought, he probably still *was* married to Velma, hard to serve the papers down here after all. Because these days Leonard did have a downtown address, not that you'd find it on any list of postal codes. It was hard to regulate mail to a cardboard box.

He'd been in the underpass a year now and had left a great deal of his old life behind. He was no longer even called Leonard Weisman. To his fellow travellers down here in this exclusive offshoot of urban existence, he was known simply as Liquid Len, due to the fact that he was a very thirsty man. Very thirsty indeed.

Liquid Len was awake that morning due to the unfortunate fact that he had barely managed to get his lips around a bottle the day before. Therefore he had not had the advantage of a good night's sleep that being screaming bloody drunk gets you. Say what you like about unconsciousness, he thought, shifting himself around underneath his threadbare blanket, but at least it keeps the bastard cold off and makes the day go by a bit quicker.

A few feet away lay Mary the Greek.

Len had no idea if Mary *was* Greek (to him she sounded kind of Irish), but that was what they all called her so to hell with it.

She was a contrary woman, prone to screaming in the middle of the night. She believed the underpass to be besieged by alien life forms and was frequently convinced they wanted to probe her with their 'evil ass pumps'. This opinion was frequently the highest source of laughter in the underpass and would keep a lot of the locals laughing right through until the early hours. By which time, they would be so drunk they'd all be trying to yank her skirts up and get out of the cold for a while. The fact that this behaviour was no doubt the cause of her paranoid delusions seemed to have slipped past everybody involved. But then the underpass was not a place for deep thinkers.

Len wondered if Mary might be of a mind for a little rough and tumble now. If nothing else, it might make him a bit more sleepy.

Then he decided he really couldn't be bothered. Len was not what you might call a romantic.

He rolled out from under his blanket and strolled off into the bushes for a piss.

This act of gentlemanly privacy was not just civility on Len's part. Truth was, he had a shy bladder and one had to keep some semblance of societal convention, even down here where the air was so thick with methane you could silence a hungry belly just by taking a deep breath.

While enjoying his morning ablutions, Len looked up past the concrete pillars and imagined who might be driving above his head. Sometimes he filled his days with this game. Gave them all names and wondered where they lived. Wondered what it would take to see them down here spending their days in a home with *Apple Jacks* printed on the side.

Not much he reckoned, not much at all.

He zipped himself up and decided to go for a stroll, work out the aches in his legs.

At 8.14 he looked up and saw the Channel 7 helicopter hovering above them all. In a moment of absurd solemnity, he saluted it. He had no idea why.

Gleason let the fronds of the Ytraxorian rifle close over his hand. Rather than be unnerved by the tingle of electricity, he decided to be emboldened by it. He imagined that charge coursing up his arm, making his heart pound faster, filling him with life and determination. He opened his heart to the weapon, let it see all he had to give, let it know how far he was willing to go, how little mercy was to be found in him.

It began to hum.

It was hungry.

It wanted to see a world *burn*.

Gleason pointed it at the coursing lanes of traffic below and pulled the trigger.

The effect was not instantaneous.

A laser beam did not scythe down bringing instant death.

The force that blossomed from the barrel of the gun was slow, almost lethargic. It floated down like a cloud of pollen rather than a wave of energy. The quality of the light changed when viewed through it, a crystal clarity, like that found just before a storm.

'Jazz hands!' cried Larry Gulliver, eager to see his wonderful son wave those delicate, heartbreaking fingers at him. Fingers he just wanted to kiss whenever he laid eyes on them. Then he saw the back of his own hands and the effect the almost imperceptible wave had on them. They grew paler, drier, Fat brown splotches grew between the lengthening grey hairs, liver spots enlarging like droplets of wine soaking into a cream table cloth. He held his hands up towards him, mindless of the road ahead, and watched them crumble from the fingertips down. Like the perfect ash of a cigarette crumbled away to nothing at the whisper of a breeze.

He turned to his son, to make sure he was OK, but the rest of his body followed his hands and all he succeeded in doing was spraying the backseat of the car with the soft, fatty ash of his face.

Car collided with car, bumper meeting bumper, as every driver experienced the same thing. Some had the foresight to slam a foot down on the brake, but the crumbling bones of their ankles couldn't bear up to such strain and powdered with the impact. Passengers stared open-mouthed only realising that the same desiccation was visited upon them as their startled eyes wizened and wept out of their sockets to push loose the powdery flesh of their cheeks.

Liquid Len, looking up and watching that faint wave as it fell down on them all, bringing years of age as it passed, had a little longer than most to wonder what it was that had brought all the traffic crashing to a slow halt. He heard the crump of compacted metal and the tinkle of shattered glass, almost graceful as the slow, rush-hour chain, hundreds and hundreds of lives, came to a halt above his head.

Then the wave hit him also and his salute, still in place, crumbled down into confused eyes. His last thought was an apologetic one. All these years, he thought, and Mary the Greek was right after all.

A peace descended, broken only by the constant shuffle of the helicopter blades as Gleason and Mulroney descended for a flyby. Mulroney held the camcorder with one hand, the control stick for the helicopter with the other. As they flew past, he let the camera's lens linger on as much of the carnage as possible. They circled a few times until, with the distant sound of traffic sirens creeping ever closer, they decided enough was enough and sailed away to clear skies.

Below, car after car sat stationary on the Interstates. Those that were outside of the field of fire drew to a halt as they looked at the chaos in front of them, a chaos that spanned half a mile in all directions.

As the emergency vehicles pushed their way through, they moved from car to car, unable to believe what they saw. Every vehicle empty but for the ageing, crumbled remains of people, most no more recognisable than the emptied bags of vacuum cleaners.

Then a call rang out in the unnaturally still Denver morning. 'Over here,' came a woman's voice. 'I've got one!'

Sergeant Dolores Cortez, of the Denver Police Department, couldn't believe the look of the guy sitting naked on the back seat of the car. Hand over her mouth, she wondered if it was cancer that made him look the way he did. He was so thin, every vein visible through his translucent skin. It's not cancer, she realised as she opened the door and backed off to let him crawl out. He was just so old.

Why wasn't he walking, she wondered, knowing she should reach out and help him up. But the old guy just wailed and Cortez couldn't deal with that, however much it shamed her.

'Sir?' she said. 'Sir, what happened here?'

But young Mikey Gulliver had never learned to talk, and all he could do was cry for his father, both hands splayed out towards her.

Jazz hands.

Eighteen

To begin with, the TV news kept playing the same, flat footage: an aerial sweep of the Mousetrap, showing lengths of crashed cars. After a while, they stopped. However much the anchors talked the situation up, there was no story until they found a face. Finally, they found a family member who was happy to cry on screen. She would become a media star for a week or so, while the rolling voice of America waffled away beneath her on a scrolling banner of texts, emails and tweets. Needless to say, the majority of comments would deplore the Muslims who had likely perpetrated this horror. The news networks would be happy not to correct them, as would the government. Many extremist groups would also be happy to take the credit for the awful loss of life. Eventually, an easy target (the Freedom Voice of America, a white-supremacist movement run from a bus depot in Michigan) would be selected for the prize. The security services knew where to find them and, once assured that there would be no more unpleasant incidents, they would release proof of the Freedom Voice of America's involvement and promptly smack them hard, live on camera. And while that blatant piece of misdirection was going on, they would mop up after the real cause of what was now being called the 'Rush Hour Massacre'. They would do it quietly, ruthlessly and with no mention whatsoever of the truth.

They would particularly not mention Mr Wynter, currently sat on a bench overlooking the Constitutional Gardens Pond, not a heavily vetted stone's throw from the White House.

He was eating sushi from a polystyrene box. He hated its cold, bland flavour, but his doctor had given him strict instructions to cut down on red meat. He had been allowing himself a few indulgences too many. Oh, to still have a young man's constitution.

'Two meetings on one operation,' said the voice behind him. 'Both with their fair share of recrimination.'

Mr Wynter had no need to turn around. He knew his employer's voice well enough. Besides, when meeting in public it was common form to avoid eye contact, just two gentlemen strolling in the park looking at the ducks. Mr Wynter imagined most of the park's strollers were secretly plotting the downfall of governments. Spies were amongst the most predictable people on earth.

'There has been more than the usual amount of ill-fortune in this matter,' Mr Wynter agreed. 'But I am confident that it will soon be resolved.'

'Oh, you're confident, are you? Well, that's a

relief. I wake up to a shit-storm of dead motorists on the news but you're confident it'll all be fine.'

'Don't pretend a few fatalities matter,' Mr Wynter replied. 'You know as well as I do that, with enough spin, Gleason did you a favour. There's nothing the voting public like better than a strong government, smacking down the aggressor. If the Republicans had their way, you'd be paying people like me to kill that many civilians *every* week.'

'Your age has made you so cynical.'

'It has made me *aware*.'

'One hopes it has made you sufficiently wise to finally resolve matters. Just in case, I feel it's only fair to warn you that there have been discussions as to your possible replacement.' There was a long pause at that. 'Perhaps, in truth, we should have done it years ago. A man can only fight for so many years.'

'Some of us can do nothing else,' Mr Wynter replied.

'Then I look forward to your proving as much.'

Mr Wynter stared at the ducks for a few more moments, allowing his employer time to walk away. He popped another piece of sushi in his mouth. It tasted of compromise.

'I think I just heard my career roll over and die,' said Rex, sat next to Shaeffer on a red-eye from Colorado Springs to Washington.

Shaeffer spun the ice in his plastic glass of scotch and coke, trying to make its coldness infect the tepid fizz of the soda. 'I think it was just wind from that guy three rows behind us. The one that's going to force me to kill him with a rolled-up inflight magazine if he snores any louder.'

'Excuse me,' came an irritated voice from behind them. 'Would you mind keeping it down? I'm trying to sleep.'

'Tell that to the Manatee with allergies in seat 4B,' Shaeffer replied.

'We're discussing governmental business,' said Rex, poking his face between the seats. 'Matters of international security. I suggest you ask the stewardess for earplugs, as I will have to have you deported as a security risk if I think you've been listening in.'

'You're drunk.'

'Damn right I am. There's nothing I won't do in the name of my country. Now wrap that blanket around your head and go to sleep.'

The passenger mumbled to herself but turned over and pretended to doze off.

'You really think there's nothing we can do?' Schaeffer asked.

Rex shrugged. 'Who knows where he is? Unless he slips up – and he doesn't seem like the kind of guy that does – we're only ever going to hear where he's *been*.'

'And when we do hear that...'

'Then it means we've blown it. Again.' Rex shuffled in his seat and gestured towards the flight attendant for another pair of drinks. 'Not that it matters. After the last few days, I'm about as popular as Gleason. I've been acting way out of my remit and I've got nothing to show for it but a few expense receipts and an ex-special-forces grunt who refuses to stop following me around. At this rate, I'll be lucky to get a post filing paperwork.'

Gleason and Mulroney had found themselves overnight accommodation in a small cottage on the fringes of Arlington County. It had taken some time before they had found a suitable place, somewhere with enough private, off-road parking to stash the truck they had appropriated north of Denver. The previous inhabitants were wrapped up in bed sheets and dumped under a pile of firewood in the outhouse.

'Transporting that much stuff,' said Mulroney as they sat in the cottage's front room eating a stew that Mulroney had prepared from what he could find in the kitchen, 'it draws too much attention. We need to find somewhere remote, a new base of operations.'

'What we need to do,' Gleason replied, 'is keep the pressure on until they're forced to give in.'

Mulroney sighed and shuffled chunks of lamb around his plate. 'You really think they're going to?' he asked. 'You and I both know the standard response to terror threats. What makes you think this is going to be different?'

'Scale,' said Gleason. 'We're going to hit them so hard, so publicly, that they'll be begging for a way to make it stop.'

Mulroney shrugged. 'Ask me, it'd be a hell of a lot easier just to sell the weaponry off. It's not like it would be difficult to find a buyer. Hell, most of our professional life has been building a list of contacts. A nice, quiet private sale and we vanish off the radar. Wouldn't that be better?'

'I'm not handing weapons like this over to the enemies of America.'

Mulroney almost laughed. 'You suddenly found a streak of patriotism?'

Gleason gave him a look that made it quite clear Mulroney had gone too far.

'I never lost it,' he said. 'I wish I could say the same of our leaders.'

Mulroney raised his hands in a placatory gesture. 'OK, so we don't sell outside the country. Forget I mentioned it.'

Later, as he was fetching the video camera, Mulroney began to wonder if there was an escape route open for him. He'd always known Gleason was a little flaky round the edges, liked the feel of a trigger too much. But, in truth, Mulroney could relate to that and, over the years, the pair of them had looked after each other and built a future for themselves in case they ever wanted to leave the life behind. But now Mulroney's future was compromised. When he'd abandoned his ranch, he'd also been leaving all the money he had hidden there over the years – if anyone were to dig in his vegetable patch, they would find a far richer crop than potatoes. The chain of vacuum jars filled with banknotes had grown vast. That loss was acceptable when he had believed it would be replaced – and more – by the spoils of their current actions. Now he wasn't sure he believed any such thing.

Gleason wasn't in this for the money. When

they had flown over the Mousetrap in Denver, Mulroney had seen the relish on the man's face as he looked down on the destruction. Gleason had fallen in love with the power these weapons offered. Mulroney wasn't convinced he'd give them up for any price. He thought Gleason would hold on to them until there was nobody left to point them at. Which left Mulroney as little more than a future target, and that was something he had been working to avoid once and for all.

He took the camera through to Gleason. 'You ready?'

Gleason nodded and Mulroney began to record.

'Wise Men of America,' Gleason began. 'I have once again proven our power over you.' Mulroney began to zone out, Gleason's speeches were beginning to take on the air of the zealot, not the voice of a business proposal but the sabre-rattling of a vengeful god. He kept the camera steady and began to wonder how he might extricate himself from all of this.

'This will be my final demonstration,' Gleason continued. 'One that will strike at the very heart of your corrupt, shadow-puppet government. When we talk again, it will be your one and only chance to make this end. Think about that, and make your decision wisely.'

Gleason nodded, and Mulroney stopped recording.

'You want me to send it straightaway?'

'Of course,' said Gleason. 'Let them have a few hours to be afraid. Then get some sleep, we've got one hell of a day tomorrow and we'll need to be sharp.'

'Roger that,' Mulroney replied.

The message was sent, received and discussed, nowhere more exhaustively than in a small room in a shabby-looking office block in downtown Washington. The office block was registered to a toy company that specialised in pre-school learning games, but the major shareholders had no interest in colourful plastic bricks or large, wooden animals. They just liked having somewhere innocuous to meet that paid for itself.

'So what do we do?' asked the man Mr Wynter would have recognised as his employer. 'Wait for him to make his move?'

'Unless your man has any better ideas, I don't see that we have much choice,' an older voice replied.

'Have we no clue as to Gleason's location?' asked a woman sat near the window. She was watching her car parked below, convinced that somebody would steal it while she had left it unattended.

'He must be in the vicinity of Washington,' said another voice, a young man with a hint of an Irish accent, 'given his target.'

'The real question,' said the older man, 'is what we do with him when he does make his move. What deal are we willing to offer?'

'I've been thinking about that,' said Mr Wynter's employer, 'and it occurred to me that we might want to offer him a job.'

*

Rex woke to an overcast Washington morning and a hangover that loitered at the back of his forehead and waited to pounce. His phone was ringing, which, in those first cumbersome moments of waking, seemed entirely unreasonable on its part.

'Yeah?'

'Jesus, Rex.' It was Esther. 'You sound rough.'

'Feel it, too. What can I do for you? You got some coffee orders I need to work on? Or maybe some mopping up around Langley?'

'Mopping up hits it. I shouldn't be telling you this, officially you're no longer in the loop, but there's been another video from Gleason.'

'Because watching that bastard gloat will improve my morning no end.'

'There's something else.' Esther's genuine excitement was finally overcoming her insecurities, Rex could hear it in her voice, even over the sound of his own pulsing temples and churning stomach. 'We've had communication from Mulroney. He wants to cut a deal.'

On his way to the shower, Rex woke Shaeffer. He'd let the man stay over, neither of them being sober enough to even conceive of booking a hotel room.

'Get your head straight,' he shouted. 'Make coffee, make breakfast... today will be a good day.'

'I'm having trouble believing that,' Shaeffer admitted, rubbing his face. There was a burst of water as the shower came to life, and he shuffled through to the kitchen. He put the coffee machine on then stuck his head in the cooler. It felt nice in there, he was almost tempted to rest his cheek on a pack of bacon and snooze for a while under the soft orange light. Instead, he decided to see if he could drink all the juice he could find, a challenge as well as a restorative.

By the time Rex got out of the shower, Shaeffer was feeling marginally better. His mouth was no longer filled with what had felt like dead slugs. 'What's all the excitement, then?' he asked.

'We've had contact from Gleason and Mulroney,' said Rex, '*separately*. Gleason is dishing out the usual threats, Mulroney wants out. Looks like we may have a chance to stop this bastard, after all.'

'What's the deal?'

'Mulroney wants immunity and cash, nothing too inventive.'

'All the more believable. He say why?'

'He's convinced Gleason doesn't want to deal, thinks the power's gone to his head.'

'I could believe that, too. So what's the next step?'

'The security service is waiting on a location from Mulroney. He's given them the number of a cellphone that he intends to turn on once he's ready to be picked up.'

'What? And he's just trusting them not to shoot him on sight?'

'I guess he doesn't think he has much choice.'

Shaeffer shrugged. 'Maybe, just doesn't sound like the Mulroney I know. So what's this got to do with us? Even if you were still popular with your section chief, which you're not, this isn't CIA.'

'Yeah.' Rex grabbed some coffee and tried to hide his irritation. 'But that doesn't mean the CIA can't tag along.'

'Have we at least got an idea what the target will be?'

'A pretty good one. Remember what you said about striking at the heart of America?'

Shaeffer nodded. Rex turned his phone towards him and played the media file Esther had sent.

'Wise Men of America,' said Gleason, staring into the camera, 'I have once again proven our power over you. Now I come for your leader. Please,' Gleason smiled, 'raise your armies, do your best to stop me. But I promise you – within twenty-four hours, he and his loved ones will be dead. That will be my final demonstration. One that will strike at the very heart of your corrupt, shadow-puppet government. When we talk again, it will be your one and only chance to make this end. Think about that, and make your decision wisely.'

The video ended and Rex put his phone away. 'Not a lot of ambiguity there,' he said. 'The nut-job's planning to assassinate the president.'

Nineteen

Gleason and Mulroney woke early and prepared for the drive into the capital.

Gleason had decided they should take the cottage owners' car rather than the truck. It was good to keep switching vehicles, and this time he had no intention of taking everything with them. The key was to travel light, get in and out of the theatre of operations and be on the move before the enemy even had time to react. He spent twenty minutes cherry-picking equipment from the weaponry crates, packing them into a long shoulder bag and storing them on the backseat of the car.

'OK,' he said to Mulroney, 'time to get moving.'

Mulroney nodded and reached for the car keys.

'It's all right,' said Gleason. 'I'll drive.'

Mulroney thought about arguing but could tell it would be pointless – Gleason was in no mood to negotiate. Today was set in stone. He ran his thumb across the pocket of his jeans, feeling the solid rectangle of the phone he had stashed there. He'd found it in the house and, like Shaeffer before him, had recognised it for what it was: a slim line of escape. At the moment it was turned off, but if at any point he decided that should change... He now had an escape route.

They drove past Arlington cemetery, and Gleason looked out over the rows and rows of dead soldiers, wondering how many he had put there.

'You're quiet this morning,' said Mulroney, cutting through Gleason's thoughts and bringing his attention back to the road. 'Having second thoughts?'

'Never,' Gleason replied. 'Can you say the same?'

Mulroney shrugged. 'I have doubts,' he admitted. 'Of course I do. Who doesn't when they're going off to fight?' *Especially when they're not sure what they're fighting for,* he thought.

Gleason nodded slightly, pushing the car along Memorial Bridge. They cruised over the Potomac River, a morning sun bouncing off the water in crystalline explosions of white light, like the distant flashes of a strafe run in the desert. Gleason imagined the sound of shellfire, the soft crump of ignition and the spray of bricks and earth. He would bring that here. Turn this green and white slice of heritage and navel-gazing into a place of flame and noise, a timely reminder of the reality of war.

'Can I trust you, Mulroney?' he asked, his voice deceptively gentle. He had known the man many years and had never had to ask that question. But now he did. Because there was a look in Mulroney's eyes, a mixture of fear and deception. It was the look of a man who said what he thought others wanted to hear. Gleason knew that face, had seen it writ large in countless battlefield interrogations. The placatory look of a man who knows his time is almost at hand.

'Why are you even asking me that?' asked Mulroney. 'After all the years we've served together you don't know the answer?'

'I always did,' Gleason said quietly. 'But today's war is a little different.'

Damn right it is, thought Mulroney, it's war for the hell of it. He made a snap decision and slipped his hand into his pocket to turn on the phone.

'We're outnumbered,' he said, 'and they're prepared for us. We're fighting for a vague promise of cash. More likely we'll end up bleeding out in the middle of Constitution Gardens. Yeah, Cotter, this war is different. I thought we were in this for the money! But you don't care about that, do you?'

'There are more important things than money.'

'Yeah,' Mulroney agreed, 'there are, and maybe if you asked me to risk my life for them then I would. But this isn't even about principles, this is just about pulling the trigger for the hell of it. Somewhere – and maybe it's since you started playing with that freaky goddamn rifle you love so much – you've got yourself all turned around. You've lost perspective. Cotter, you're not the man you once were.' Mulroney paused. 'Or maybe this is what you always were,' he said finally. 'I don't know.'

They drove in silence for a moment, Mulroney looking down in his lap, Gleason staring straight ahead at the Lincoln Memorial as it rose up ahead of them. A monument to a dead president, Gleason thought. They'll need another one in about an hour.

The phone in Mulroney's pocket began to ring.

Mulroney just stared at his pocket for a second, utterly disbelieving his misfortune. Then he reached for his gun. Gleason was quicker – despite his age, he usually was.

They drove on, Gleason steering gently around the memorial. 'Answer it,' he said.

'It's not my phone,' said Mulroney. Realising how stupid that sounded, he tried to elaborate. 'I picked it up at the cottage, that's all, Thought it might be useful.' The phone's answer machine took the call, the ringing finally stopping. 'Look,' said Mulroney, 'I'll get it out, you can take a look, it'll just be someone wanting to speak to, well… whoever the hell it was that owned that house.'

Mulroney held the phone out to Gleason, nearly dropping it as it began to ring again. Gleason placed his gun in his lap and took the phone. 'I believe you,' he said. 'Now maybe we both need to calm down a little.'

Mulroney lowered his own gun and Gleason answered the call.

'Mr Gleason?' asked a voice.

Gleason kept his face impassive as he answered. 'Yeah.'

'This is a representative of the United States Government.'

'That so?'

'Indeed. Might I suggest you dismiss your subordinate? It can't be a great surprise to learn he has sold you out. That is why I have this number. He gave it to us so we could trace your movements. For now, that trace is not happening. I have bought us a little time so that I can make a proposition to you. I imagine you will doubt that, but all I can say is this: if we just wanted to trace you why would I call and warn you of the fact? Think about that as you deal with Mr Mulroney. I shall call you back in a minute or so.'

The phone went dead before Gleason had a chance to answer. He placed the phone in his lap, moving casually.

'Well?' said Mulroney. 'Who the hell was it?'

Gleason swung his fist into Mulroney's face, breaking his nose. He snatched Mulroney's gun and, straightening the car a little before he ran it off the road, pointed it at him.

'It was for me,' said Gleason. 'Interesting, don't you think?'

'Jesus, Cotter!' Mulroney whined, blood dripping onto his lap from between the hands he cupped to his nose. 'Somebody's screwing with us, OK?'

'Really?' Cotter asked. 'That the best you've got?'

Mulroney sighed. 'OK, screw it. You were acting like a flake, what do you expect? I found myself an exit. Do what you like, I ain't begging.'

'They tracing the phone?' Gleason asked.

'Of course.'

Gleason thought about it for a moment. The man on the phone certainly had a point, if they just wanted to track him why alert him to the fact? He was not a naturally trusting man, but in this case logic dictated he hear the man out. But he would also take something else the caller had said under advice: he would continue alone.

'Damn shame,' he said to Mulroney.

'Eighteen years, man,' Mulroney replied.

'Yeah.' Gleason shot Mulroney in the temple and picked up the phone just as it began to ring.

'We alone now?' the voice asked.

'Yes,' Gleason replied. 'Now say your piece before I dump this thing.'

'Well, Mr Gleason, we'd simply like to offer you a job. We both know that this current trajectory of yours is untenable. Shoot up central Washington if you must, but where do you go from there? Do you really imagine a future where we will be wiring money into offshore bank accounts just to make you go away? That's not what we do to terrorists, Mr Gleason. We simply keep pursuing them until eventually they are dead. You know this. You are one of the blunt tools we have used to achieve this goal in the past.'

'And your alternative?'

'You come to work for us. You would be our ultimate enforcer in matters of global security. It is a select position. One that has had very few occupants.'

'And the current man in the post?'

'The gentleman that forced your location in Colorado out of David Ellroy. Unfortunately for us, some short time after you had already vacated it.'

'And how does he feel about being replaced?'

'I imagine you'll be able to ask him soon. We have held off the involvement of the security service. They are still loitering around the parks of central Washington waiting for a viable cellphone trace to lead them to you.'

'Whereas your man?'

'Is already en route.'

'Lying son of a bitch.'

'Not at all, the offer is genuine as long as you are the last man standing. If you agree to take the post, you will be cared for for the rest of your life, given free rein to indulge your tastes and act as our singular global enforcer. We may even let you keep some of the weaponry, though, naturally, our people would like to study it a little first.'

'Cared for for the rest of my life?'

'Indeed, every comfort will be afforded you. We treat our employees well, Mr Gleason.'

'Up until you choose to replace them.'

There was a slight pause at that. 'Do you want the job or not?'

'I'll let you know.'

Gleason threw the phone out of his window and watched as it splintered beneath the wheels of the car behind him.

Ahead, where Constitution Drive continued through the parks, a large barrier was erected. No great surprise there, Gleason thought. Easy enough to arrange and who cares if you piss off a few tourists? There was a sign on the barrier: 'Warning – Gas Leak', it declared.

Gleason turned left, continuing up 17th Street, running parallel to the park. He passed the White House and continued on, noting the ring of barriers and the security staff. When he was able to pull off the road, he did so, yanking Mulroney's dead body forward so his head leaned on the dashboard. He had a bottle of water in the compartment of his door and he pulled it out, unscrewing the cap and splashing it on the passenger window to clean off the worst of the blood. People didn't pay that much attention, he decided, and security had enough area to cover without checking out all the cars in the vicinity.

He reached for the long bag on the back seat and pulled it forward onto his lap. He wouldn't need as much of this as he had hoped. Just one man left standing.

He pulled out a small box of wires and glass attached to the pocket of a rucksack. Leaning forward, he pulled the rucksack on back to front so that the bag hung at his chest. Inside was a heavy string of D Cell batteries. There was room for a couple more handguns from the shoulder bag, so he added them and then zipped the rucksack up. Last of all, he gripped the Ytraxorian rifle and pressed a switch nestled in the centre of the box of wires. There was a quiet whine as it powered up from the batteries and he stepped out of the car. As he moved over to the sidewalk, an old man walked right into him. Of course, Gleason thought, dodging the oncoming pedestrians who made no attempt to step out of his way. It's working, he realised, they don't notice me. The rucksack was a portable perception filter, a device that didn't render the wearer invisible but convinced those around not to notice. Its effect was fragile: draw too much attention and it would stop working altogether, but as long as he walked slowly and made no sudden movements it should give him all the advantage he needed.

He walked back along the road, heading down Pennsylvania Avenue where the pedestrians thinned out to be replaced by the barriers and the fake gas-leak warnings. Gleason found a spot between groups of security staff – he didn't want to try this directly under their noses – and pushed his way past the barrier and off the road. Nobody looked towards him. He began to walk along the grass, heading straight for the rear of the White House.

The area was thick with uniformed security services, gathered together into groups or walking in pairs around the periphery keeping their eyes peeled for someone suspicious. But he wasn't suspicious, was he? He wasn't even here...

He walked slowly, not even wanting to run in case that was enough to compromise the effect of the perception filter.

As he got closer, he felt the fronds of the Ytraxorian gun close around his hands, that electric tingle spreading up to his elbows.

Was it as easy as this? he wondered. No doubt, once he started firing, people would pay more attention. But by then it would be far too late.

Was there nobody to stop him?

'We can recognise your man on sight!' insisted Rex, exasperated at the security services' lack of interest in either his or Shaeffer's presence.

'Thanks to a miraculous new gadget called a camera, so can we.'

Max Scott, chief of the uniformed secret service policemen – and man most likely to have a severe migraine by midday – had little patience for interdepartmental interference. He had enough on his plate without agents from other agencies getting under his feet. The President, against Scott's advice, was refusing to evacuate. Apparently, he didn't want to send a message of 'no trust' in those charged to protect him. 'Besides,' he had said when the emergency meeting drew to a close, 'it's just one guy, right?'

'If you want my opinion,' Scott said to Rex, 'and you're going to get it whether you do or not, this whole situation is going to wind up being a false alarm.' He held up his arm to stop Rex arguing. 'And if it isn't, I have several hundred uniformed officers and special agents waiting to catch this whacko and throw him into a cell.'

'Look,' said Rex, 'I know you guys can do your jobs. I'm just asking that you let us be involved. As a courtesy.'

'In my line of work, courtesies are few and far between. You're in my way, and I don't need you. Get beyond the security barrier and stay there.'

Scott marched away leaving a small detail of

officers to escort Rex and Shaeffer back to the road.

'Great,' Rex sighed. 'So we're left circling the perimeter, hoping we get lucky.'

'You expect a man who's trained to infiltrate and execute to stick to the sidewalk?' asked Shaeffer. 'It's not really my style.'

'Tough. If we break in, all we're going to do is draw fire away from Gleason. The last thing they need is two targets to divide up their forces.'

'Point.'

They walked up 17th Street, feeling utterly redundant as they tried to survey the parkland through the trees.

Gleason waited until he was about twenty feet from the White House, raised the rifle and cleared his mind of everything but the intent to do damage.

Just as it had above the Denver traffic, a wide field of almost entirely transparent energy flowed from the barrel of the gun and spread out towards the building. Gleason squeezed the rifle tight in his hands, let the electric caress of the seaweed fronds cover him from head to foot. He returned energy of his own, channelling the fear and anger of every battlefield he had ever experienced back into the rifle and out of the barrel.

He heard shouting from his left. Here they come, he thought, *finally*. He released the trigger, letting the cloud of energy roll towards the building as he turned his fire on the security services that were running towards him. He experimented, telling the rifle what he wanted it to do as it coughed bursts of energy through the air towards his attackers. Some of the men vanished; others crumbled to dust. The more he fired, the more the air seemed to alter around him. Time itself seemed to slow, the air becoming a thing of liquid. Noises distorted, becoming low, bass roars.

The wave of energy struck the building and cracks radiated outward, as if it had been hit by a hammer. The effect crept wider and wider, rolling over walls, creeping up pillars, blacking out windows.

Gleason felt the world draw slower still as all around him men fell or vanished.

He felt weak. That electric numbness creeping over him as he sank to his knees, the rifle drooping and sending a wedge of grass deathly yellow as it touched the ground.

In front of him, the White House finally fell, toppling inwards like a controlled demolition, walls falling, glass cracking. Plumes of brick dust erupting upwards. There was screaming, those low, slow voices speeding up now the rifle was powering down. The world was a record finding its correct spin speed. Nobody came near him now, all staring at the utter destruction of the iconic residence before them. Bodies were viewable in the wreckage but they were as decaying and aged as the stone that piled around them.

'Got you, you bastard,' said Gleason.

His breath was short and he could barely raise his head as he saw an old man walk up to him. The man was wearing a light-grey suit that was almost as out of place amongst this destruction as the smile on his face. He recognised the old man's face, had seen him somewhere recently... Then he remembered: it was the man he had bumped into after stepping out of the car.

'Well, Mr Gleason,' said Mr Wynter. 'I imagine you must be rather pleased with yourself? Today can, after all, be considered something of a success.'

The old man reached down and pulled the rifle out of Gleason's hands. Try as he might, the old soldier couldn't resist.

'Don't worry,' said Mr Wynter, 'the nerve agent I spiked you with during our earlier collision isn't permanent.' He gave Gleason a smile. 'When you're my age, you take all the advantages you can get.'

This is him, Gleason thought, this is the enforcer... the man they wanted me to replace.

'Fascinating, isn't it?' Mr Wynter continued, looking at the rifle. 'A weapon that responds to the potential of who wields it.' He gave a chuckle. 'Just wait until it sinks its teeth into me!'

The gun pulsed brightly as the weed fronds closed around Mr Wynter's old hands.

Mr Wynter sighed, quite taken aback by the energy that pulsed through him. 'Oh yes...' he said. 'That really is something else, isn't it?'

Gleason mumbled something, still not able to speak.

'What was that?' Mr Wynter asked, leaning in close.

'Get on with it,' Gleason whispered. 'Shoot me.'

Mr Wynter laughed. 'Now why would I do something as stupid as that?' he asked.

He turned the rifle on himself and pulled the trigger.

Nineteen

Rex and Shaeffer drove into central Washington and parked a short walk away from the Washington Monument.

'You going to have any sway getting in here?' Shaeffer asked. 'I mean, at least tell me we're not going to get shot by our own people the minute we stray too close?'

'You think I should have brought my special, pink CIA T-shirts so they knew who we were?'

They came to the barrier and Rex waved at one of the men loitering around the railings trying to look like a gas engineer.

'Hey,' he called. 'Rex Matheson, CIA.' He dangled his ID as the man walked over. 'Now obviously you just work for the gas company, but can you tell your foreman that I have someone who has worked alongside Gleason for years, knows his methods, can recognise him on sight and, as such, should really be on the same side of the barrier as you?'

The man in the overalls stared at him in confusion for a moment.

'*Now*, if you would,' said Rex. 'If the President gets himself assassinated while we're all stood here playing with our dicks, I'll feel we've had a wasted morning.'

The man snatched Rex's ID and walked away, pulling a radio out of the pocket of his overalls. Glancing up and down the road, he began to talk into the radio, his back turned to Rex and Shaeffer.

'Subtle move,' said Shaeffer. 'How long do you think it'll take for us both to be escorted over the city limits?'

'He's secret service,' said Rex, 'and I'm banking on the fact that the secret service hasn't the first idea who we are and likely won't care.' He smiled at Shaeffer. 'You always think you're the centre of attention? It would take the gasman over there several hours of interdepartmental cross-checks just to find out your surname. He's going to check with his boss, and as long as neither of us are red-flagged as security risks we should at least get on the other side of that fence.'

The man returned and waved them past the barrier. 'Chief wants to talk to you.'

'I just bet he does,' said Rex, grinning at Shaeffer. 'Where's he at?'

The man in the overalls led them to the Ellipse, where a group of uniformed security services men stood waiting.

'You the CIA guy?' asked one of them.

'You the man in charge?' Rex replied.

'Only CIA would have the lack of manners to answer a question with a question,' the man replied. 'Max Scott, Chief of Police. What's this I hear about you knowing this guy?'

'We've been tracking him for a few days,' said Rex. 'This is a former member of his unit, been helping us since the rest went rogue.'

'Glen Shaeffer.' Shaeffer stuck out his hand, but Scott ignored it.

'Want to tell me what you're doing here?' he asked. 'Nobody told me to expect a CIA presence. Which they sure as hell would have if this were any of your business.'

'We just want to help out, sir,' said Rex. 'Offer whatever assistance we can and see this business through until the end.'

'You're a little out of your jurisdiction, son,' said Scott, 'and I fail to see what use you can be to me.'

'We can recognise your man on sight!' insisted Rex, exasperated at the security services' lack of interest in either his or Shaeffer's presence.

'Thanks to a miraculous new gadget called a camera, so can my men. If you want my opinion, and you're going to get it whether you do or not, this whole situation is going to wind up being a false alarm, and if it isn't I have several hundred uniformed officers and special agents waiting to catch this whack job and throw him into a cell.'

'Look,' said Rex, 'I know you guys can do your jobs. I'm just asking that you let us be involved. As a courtesy.'

'In my line of work, courtesies are few and far between,' said Scott. 'You're in my way, and I don't need you. Get beyond the security barrier and stay there.' He reached to his ear as he received a cellphone call. He tapped the earpiece to answer and listened as the person on the other end talked at him. 'But sir...' he said, trying to restore a little authority before the caller snatched it away again. He didn't manage any more, the voice talking over him. 'Understood,' said Scott eventually, realising that there was not much to do but accept. 'OK, sir, every courtesy, yes.'

He looked to Rex and Shaeffer. 'Now you two are really pissing me off,' he said. 'I've just had orders to grant you full access. So,' he gestured towards the White House, 'knock yourselves out. Just don't get in the way of me or my men.'

'Thank you,' said Rex with a big smile. 'It's been great working with such a cooperative guy. A real pleasure.'

'Go and hide in the bushes,' Scott shouted after them. 'I hope my men shoot you by accident.'

'Nice guy,' said Rex as they made their way through the President's Park towards the White House. 'Maybe I could apply to join the secret service instead? I'd love it if he was my boss.'

'You'd have such fun taking pot shots at one another over a breakfast coffee,' agreed Shaeffer.

'So,' said Rex as they reached the front lawn of the White House, 'if you were going to attack, which direction would you come from?' He began to circle the building.

'I take it the air force are vigilant on the no-fly zone?'

'Nobody gets anywhere near the air above our heads on a normal day,' Rex replied. 'I think we can safely assume that goes double for today. Aggressive-looking moths are likely to draw missile fire right now.'

Rex's cellphone began to ring. He tapped his headset to answer it.

'Good morning, Mr Matheson,' the caller said. 'May I suggest you and Mr Shaeffer head around the back of the building. I think you'll find your target is planning to approach from that direction.'

'Who the hell is this?' asked Rex, pulling his cell out of his jacket pocket to check the caller ID. The number was withheld.

Whoever it was hung up.

'What?' asked Shaeffer.

'We need to check out the rear,' said Rex, breaking into a run.

'Says who?' asked Shaeffer as they ran.

'I'm not sure,' Rex admitted, 'but unless it was Gleason himself trying to throw us off the scent...'

'Not really his style.'

'No, so we may as well take the tip and to hell with where it comes from for now.'

As they cleared the rear of the building, they both saw Gleason walking slowly towards them.

'Jesus,' said Rex, 'can you believe the balls on this guy? He just walks right in?' He drew his weapon and aimed it at Gleason. 'Drop the rifle!' he shouted.

Gleason looked towards him. 'You can see me?'

'Yeah, clever huh? Now drop the gun or I put a hole in you.'

'No,' Gleason replied, pointing the rifle at Rex and firing. Rex fell backwards for a moment before vanishing, his gun falling to the soft grass with a thud.

Shaeffer went next, his skin crumbling even as he raised his gun to fire. Dead fingers fell to dust, no longer able to hold the weight of the gun. He fell forward and exploded on the ground.

Gleason turned the rifle back towards the White House and fired.

As it crumbled, Mr Wynter watched from the shade of a distant tree, the Ytraxorian rifle in one hand and his cellphone in the other.

'Well now,' he said. 'That wasn't much use, was it?'

With a sigh, he turned the gun on himself and fired once more.

Nineteen

'We can recognise your man on sight!' insisted Rex, exasperated at the security services' lack of interest in either his or Shaeffer's presence.

'Thanks to a miraculous new gadget called a camera so can my men!' Scott replied before his earpiece crackled and he shut up in order to take the call.

'But sir…' he said before shutting up again as the person on the other end continued talking. 'Understood,' said Scott eventually. 'OK sir, every courtesy, yes.'

He turned back to Rex and Shaeffer. 'Now you two are really pissing me off,' he said. 'I've just had orders to grant you full access. So,' he gestured towards the White House, 'knock yourselves out. Just don't get in the way of me or my men.'

'Thank you,' said Rex with a big smile. 'It's been so great working with such a cooperative guy. A real pleasure.'

'Go and hide in the bushes,' Scott shouted after them. 'I hope my men shoot you by accident.'

'Nice guy,' said Rex as they made their way through the President's Park towards the White House. 'Maybe I could apply to join the secret service instead? I'd love it if he was my boss.'

The area was thick with uniformed security services, gathered together into groups or walking in pairs around the periphery keeping their eyes peeled for someone suspicious. But Gleason wasn't suspicious, was he? He wasn't even here...

He walked slowly, not even wanting to run in case that was enough to lose the effect of the perception filter.

As he got closer, he felt the fronds of the Ytraxorian gun close around his hands, that electric tingle spreading up to his elbows.

Was it as easy as this? he wondered. No doubt once he started firing, people would start to pay more attention. But by then it would be far too late.

Was there nobody to stop him?

Mr Wynter, standing only a few feet away, kept pressing the trigger on the Ytaxor gun but found it refused to respond.

'What's wrong with you, you ridiculous weapon?' Wynter moaned.

It fizzed in his hands and he felt a mental image crystallise in his head.

'I can't shoot him while he's holding the rifle as I'll destroy the rifle... OK, and is this reticence a desire to avoid paradoxes or simply self-preservation?'

He watched as Gleason shot Rex and Shaeffer again and then turned his fire towards the White House itself.

'This is getting tiresome,' he sighed, turning the weapon on himself and pulling at the fronds.

Nineteen

'Good morning, Mr Matheson,' the caller said in Rex's ear. 'May I suggest you and Mr Shaeffer head around the back of the building. I think you'll find your target is planning to approach from that direction.'

'Who the hell is this?' asked Rex. He pulled the cell out of his pocket to check the caller ID. The number was withheld.

'What?' asked Shaeffer.

'We need to check out the rear,' said Rex, beginning to run.

'Says who?' asked Shaeffer following on behind.

'I'm not sure,' Rex admitted. 'But unless it was Gleason himself trying to throw us off the scent...'

'Not really his style.'

'No, so we may as well take the tip and to hell with where it comes from for now.'

At the rear of the building, they saw Gleason walking towards them.

Rex raised his gun and shouted a warning to Gleason to stop.

'Just shoot him!' came the sound of an old man's voice and, taking his eyes off Gleason for a moment, Rex saw the old man he had met in Cuba, the one who had called himself Wynter. In fact he saw him time and time again, stood under one of the trees, waving at him from just behind Gleason, over by the White House itself... It was as if he was reflected many times over and scattered around on the grass.

Then Rex saw nothing as the pulse from Gleason's rifle hit him. One second all was black, then there was a flash of light and he was falling.

He hit the dusty ground and moaned, turning onto his back and losing consciousness for a moment.

He woke up. There was a strange man looking at him, a savage... No, not even human, surely? Long hair, animal skins... reaching towards him...

Mr Wynter sat down on the grass, surrounded by the echoes of himself. Time and again he'd tried this, it just wasn't working.

He needed to go earlier, and to hell with paradoxes...

Nineteen

'I bet we don't even get close,' said Shaeffer as Rex drove along Constitution Avenue. 'I mean, seriously, security's going to be so tight right now they're walking like virgins. You really think we can just roll up and stroll in?'

'I have charm,' said Rex.

'Yeah? Why you never show it to me?'

'You are not worthy of the Rex Matheson charm. It is a special and beautiful thing, offered only to important people.'

Rex's cell rang and he tapped at his earpiece to answer the call.

'Is that Mr Matheson?'

'Speaking.'

'Excellent, this is the CIA liaison currently working with the security service teams at the White House. Tell me, are you on your way?'

'How the hell did you know that?'

'A call from a Watch Analyst – Esther Drummond?'

Esther had talked...

'Look,' said Rex, wanting to try and turn this around before it got awkward, 'we just wanted to follow through on what we started, you know?'

'I understand, Rex, no problem, it would be good to have you with us. Could you do me a small favour though?'

'Name it.'

'Whereabouts are you?'

'Constitution Drive, just a few minutes away.'

'Perfect, could you swing up 17th for me rather than head over via the monument? I need you to follow a car for me.'

Rex looked across to Shaeffer who was mouthing 'Who is it?' at him. Rex shrugged. 'Yeah, I guess.' He turned onto 17th. 'What car?'

'Look to your left, Rex.' The phone went dead in Rex's ear as he looked out of his passenger window and made eye contact with Cotter Gleason, staring at him through the blood-spattered window of a compact Ford.

'What the hell?' Rex reacted quickly, yanking the wheel to the left and ramming Gleason's car just as he saw the man raise his arm.

A gunshot punctured the roof of the Ford as Gleason's aim went high. Rex put his foot on the accelerator, pulled forward in front of the Ford and then slammed on the brakes.

'Get down!' he shouted to Shaeffer as Gleason put a bullet through their back windscreen and then followed it with the hood of his Ford.

The two cars slid a little further up 17th and drew to a halt.

Rex climbed out, waving the traffic to keep back

as he trained his handgun on the driver's seat of the Ford.

But it was empty.

Shaeffer appeared behind him. 'Where did he go?' he asked.

'Beats me,' Rex replied, circling the car even as the sound of sirens sprang up from a short distance away.

Inside the car, there was Mulroney's dead body and nothing else.

'He must have made a run for it,' said Shaeffer.

'How?' asked Rex. 'He just didn't have time.'

Shaeffer shrugged. 'He ain't there, so how else do you explain it?'

Rex holstered his handgun and waved at the approaching police vehicle. 'I don't,' he admitted.

Nineteen

'Is that Mr Matheson?' asked Mr Wynter, walking up 17th and keeping his eye on the traffic

'Speaking.'

'Excellent, this is the CIA liaison currently working with the security service teams at the White House. Tell me, are you on your way?'

'How the hell did you know that?'

'A call from a Watch Analyst – Esther Drummond?'

Mr Wynter smiled as Rex fell silent for a moment. No doubt he was convinced that he was about to get another ear-bashing from a superior. Not at all, Rex, he thought. In fact you might find your career is about to improve a little.

'Look,' said Rex, 'we just wanted to follow through what we started, you know?'

'I understand, Rex,' Mr Wynter replied. 'No problem. It would be good to have you with us. Could you do me a small favour, though?'

'Name it.'

'Whereabouts are you?'

'Constitution Drive, just a few minutes away.'

'Perfect, could you swing up 17th for me rather than head over via the monument? I need you to follow a car for me.'

There we are! Mr Wynter saw Gleason's car come into view, closely followed by Rex.

'Yeah, I guess,' said Rex as he came up alongside Gleason. 'What car?'

'Look to your left, Rex,' said Wynter and laughed at the look of surprise on Gleason's face as he realised who was alongside him.

Gleason tried to shoot but Matheson was too quick, ramming the car and spoiling his aim. He made to pull in front of Gleason.

Now, thought Wynter, holding the rifle tight to his chest. It crackled inside his mind, finally content with the perfect owner. Do your thing, thought Wynter, a quick hop and then away we go.

He vanished from the sidewalk, reappearing in the back of Gleason's car just as it slammed into Rex's car in front. Wynter was thrown against the back of the passenger seat but managed to point the rifle at Gleason who turned just as Wynter fired.

Gleason disappeared leaving Wynter sat in the car on his own. Rex would be on him any second, he had to be quick…

Wynter grabbed the bag of weapons, pulled it close alongside the rifle and vanished, just as Rex stepped out of the car in front.

Rex stared at the empty car, his sidearm raised pointlessly in front of him.

Shaeffer joined him. 'Where did he go?' he asked.

'Beats me,' said Rex, working his way around the car. He completed the circle, the sound of sirens building as the police pushed their way through the traffic towards them. Inside, there was Mulroney's dead body, nothing else.

'He must have made a run for it,' said Shaeffer.

'How?' asked Rex. 'He just didn't have time.'

Shaeffer shrugged, 'He ain't there, so how else do you explain it?'

Rex holstered his gun and moved towards the approaching police car, yanking his ID from his back pocket. 'I don't,' he admitted.

And that was the fact of things. After all that, chasing Gleason and his men across oceans, all he had to show for it was two dented cars and a dead rogue operative.

His cellphone rang.

'Well done, Rex,' said a voice in his ear. 'This is your good friend Mr Wynter.'

Rex looked around, half-expecting the man to be close by, watching the action from a nearby window perhaps. 'Where the hell are you?' he asked.

'Oh,' Mr Wynter replied, 'a long way down the road. And it's not a road you want to follow, Rex, I assure you. You know, I imagined we would meet again. You know the sort of thing, suitably theatrical, a face-off in a quiet parking lot, or face to face in a diner somewhere...'

'Name the place.'

'Oh, I don't think so. If we did, I'd have to kill you and, believe it or not, I'm happier leaving you alive.'

'I am cool.'

'You're a man who has a small amount of idealism left,' said Wynter, 'and, whether you can believe it or not, that impresses me. If there were more people like you, after all, there would be no need for people like me.'

'And you'd like that?'

'Yes,' said Mr Wynter. 'I actually would. So I leave you with a little gift: a promise to tidy up after myself while I still have the authority to do so. I shall make a few calls, pull in a few favours and ensure that your career is back on track.'

'I don't need your help, pal.'

'In this business? You need all the help you can get. But this will be a small favour, don't worry – just a little housecleaning of the records. Where you go from there is up to you. Make me proud.'

Wynter chuckled and the phone went dead in Rex's ear.

'Make you proud,' Rex muttered. 'Asshole.'

With a sigh, he put on his most charming smile and held his hand out towards the advancing police officers.

Mr Wynter sat amongst the trees that surrounded the Holocaust memorial and looked down at the bag of weapons.

'Fascinating,' he said. 'But nobody gets to play with you, it's time the world became simpler again.'

He pointed the Ytraxorian rifle at the bag and turned it into dust.

'And as for you...' He looked at the rifle. 'Oh, I know you don't want to go anywhere.' And this was true, he could feel the semi-sentience of the thing, crawling around inside his head, filling it with impressions. 'Still, it would be better were I to look after you, don't you think?' It buzzed its reply, a warm, affirmative glow. 'Good. But before we pack you away for a little while, perhaps just a couple more tasks...'

Mr Wynter's employer was sat in the small room above the toy company offices. He was tired and the last thing he wanted was to have the meeting he had just arranged; in truth, he didn't even think it was necessary. Gleason had been missing now for weeks, with no word from him. There had been no threats, no demands. The general assumption was that he had finally lost his bottle and made a run for it. Taking the weapons, unfortunately, but it was only a matter of time before they found their way back on the open market. Then they would be bought, and things would finally be as they should.

Not the ending they had hoped for, but one far better than many of the alternatives.

There was a knock on the door.

The man sighed. Who was this now? None of his colleagues would knock... Wasn't the place supposed to be empty at this time of night? Some eager employee burning the midnight oil he supposed.

'Come in,' he said.

The door opened, and a young man stepped in.

'Sorry to disturb you, sir,' he said, 'but there's a Mr Wynter who wishes you to come down and talk to him.'

'Mr Wynter?'

Now here was a turn-up, the man thought, he hadn't expected Wynter to get in touch again. Assumed he'd run off with his tail between his legs, only too aware that his time was up and that it was better to run now rather than be 'retired' later.

He got to his feet and moved over to the door. 'Down where?' he asked, pushing past the young man.

'Way down,' the young man replied, pressing the needle of a hypodermic syringe into the man's neck. 'As low as you can go.'

Mr Wynter's employer woke up a short time later, his head foggy from the after-effects of the drug.

It was dark, and for a moment he thought he was alone. Then a light clicked on, and the young man's face appeared in front of him.

'Hello,' the young man said. 'Pleasant dreams?'

'Who are you?' the prisoner asked, yanking at the handcuffs that kept him fixed to his chair.

'Oh,' said the young man, 'I've had many names, always changing, always moving. In fact,' he said, pulling himself closer and removing a knife and fork from his pocket, 'I think there's only one thing in my life that I could say was constant.'

'What's that?' the prisoner asked, though he was afraid he knew.

'Hunger,' said Mr Wynter as he leaned in close.

100,000 BC

Bent Low ran towards the shape in the distance, forcing his tired legs to move fast so they gave him speed and heat.

As he got closer, he could see that the shape was a man, though not like Bent Low. This man's skin was paler and almost hairless. He was bigger than Bent Low, a giant, and he wore strange, thin skins. He will be dead when the cold comes, thought Bent Low. Those skins will give no heat at all. Maybe he was dead already. For surely a man could not fall out of the sky and survive? He was old, Bent Low could tell from the way the colour had faded from his short hairs. But his muscles were strong, he would still be able to hunt, of that Bent Low was sure. The animals would fear a man like this if he chased them on the plain.

'Please,' the man said, though Bent Low could not understand the noise, keeping back in case the man was dangerous. 'Please...' the man continued reaching out to Bent Low, 'my name's... Cotter Gleason and...' The man looked around, that uncertain look on his face that meant what he said was not a truth. Bent Low knew that look, he felt it on his face sometimes when his young asked for more meat. 'I'm with the CIA.'

The noises meant nothing to Bent Low, they were not language as he understood it, a simple thing of question and answer that kept his tribe functioning. The members of this sky tribe were strange indeed, he thought. Then another thought occurred to him: this man was broken. Bent Low could see from its legs that it could not run. In places, the skins that covered him had torn apart showing the red of the strange man's meat beneath.

Bent Low's family were hungry, this man would just be food for the animals went night came. Why waste the meat?

Cautiously, he raised his axe and moved up behind the fallen old man of the sky tribe. He didn't think he had any tricks in him that could catch Bent Low but he wasn't about to take the risk.

The eyes of the old man went narrow and Bent Low saw the intent to strike. Stupid old man, he thought, I am not the hunter my father was, but I am still a better hunter than you. People from the sky tribe must always be hungry, he decided, if they couldn't hide their plans better than that. He sidestepped the man's attempts to grab him and brought his axe down hard and quick on the old man's head. The man from the sky tribe pushed the life out of his mouth. It passed over his wrinkled lips like the wind of winter.

Bent Low gave a little dance of pleasure before squatting down to quickly strip the strange man of his meat. He tested a small piece of it and it was good, tough but full of flavour. Bent Low filled his sack until he couldn't fit any more.

Then he began the run back to his cave and his people.

The sky had given him a gift indeed! They wouldn't be hungry now.

Not for a while at least.

Acknowledgements

Writing a book is not, as some suggest, a lonely business. Especially not one to do with *Torchwood*. This one would not have been possible without support, comments and wise suggestions from a handful of folk. Lord Gary Russell of Cardiff, of course, and the Wise King of Los Angeles, Russell T Davies, whose initial script for *Miracle Day* I absolutely did not read and utterly adore. I have signed a Non-Disclosure Agreement that certifies the fact. Never read the wonderful, thrilling, glistening thing. Not one word. Their comments both before I began writing and after I'd finished were spot on the money and gratefully received.

As always, Debs read the thing as it was coming out of my head and acted as deadline monitor ('Have you finished yet? How about now? Or now? OK, I'll be patient... Now?'). She is wonderful and just what I need to keep me on track.

Finally, without Steve Tribe there would have been no book in the first place (so if you hated it blame him). The alcohol- and tobacco-fuelled engine behind so many of these books, he took another punt on me and I will always be grateful for his trust, advice and taste in music. He is a fine chap, and everything you've heard is a jealous lie.

James Goss was absolutely no help at all.